TWEEN FICTION Y

A

The
Pictish
Child

Other Books by Jane Yolen

Tartan Magic
The Wizard's Map

Twelve Impossible Things Before Breakfast

The Young Merlin Trilogy
Passager
Hobby
Merlin

The Wild Hunt
Wizard's Hall

The Pit Dragon Trilogy
Dragon's Blood
Heart's Blood
A Sending of Dragons

The Transfigured Heart

Here There Be Dragons
Here There Be Unicorns
Here There Be Witches
Here There Be Angels
Here There Be Ghosts

TARTAN MAGIC

The Pictish Child

Jane Yolen

HARCOURT BRACE & COMPANY

San Diego   New York   London

For Robert Harris,
my Scottish consultant

Library of Congress Cataloging-in-Publication Data
Yolen, Jane.
The Pictish child /by Jane Yolen.
p. cm.
"Tartan Magic, book two."
Summary: While visiting relatives in Scotland, three children
come to the aid of a refugee from the distant past, a young Pict
girl escaping a massacre of her people.
[1. Picts—Fiction. 2. Magic—Fiction. 3. Time travel—Fiction.
4. Scotland—Fiction.] I. Title.
PZ7.Y78Phi 1999
[Fic]—dc21   99-6303
ISBN 0-15-202261-9

Text set in Galliard Old Style
Display type set in Goudy Medieval

First edition

H G F E D C B A

Printed in the United States of America

Contents

Tartan:
Plaid cloth.
In Scotland each clan
has its own distinctive pattern.

One

■■■■

Luck

Jennifer looked out the window in disbelief. What awful luck. They had been in Scotland for only five days, the first part of their summer vacation, visiting with Gran and Da—and three of those days had been full of rain.

They'd driven from the airport in a storm so fierce it had washed the tidy streets of Fairburn clean of any dust. Yesterday it had been pouring again, the rain coming down straight and then slantwise. Today the sky was slate grey, like a badly erased blackboard, and there was more rain.

They'd already spent too many hours up in the attic playing dress-up, which Peter hated but Molly loved. And lots of card games, none of which they'd ever heard of in the States, like Patience and Happy Families and Bezique—which Peter loved and Molly hated.

And, Jennifer thought miserably, *I have been stuck in the middle of every argument. It's no different than being at home. Except for the magic.*

The magic!

They had had two incredible days when magic had surrounded them like the Scottish weather. She had conveniently forgotten the fear and the terror that had accompanied those days, remembering instead only the dizzying wonder she had felt.

But now, Jennifer thought, *it's just rain, rain, rain.*

She traced the path of one drop as it slid down the window, her finger leaving a peculiar long smudge. She could see her own image faintly in the glass, the red hair almost black against the tall, dark, wet trees, the wide-set eyes that made her look permanently surprised.

"Dreech," she said, turning to the others. It was one of the few Scottish words she had really learned, and it perfectly described the day: grey and wet and dreary. "A dreech day."

"Och, child," Gran said as she cleared away the breakfast dishes, "this day is hardly dreech. A drop or two, that's all. And with your parents and Da off to Edinburgh on business, it is just the perfect kind of day for us to go and cheer up my friends at the Eventide Home. You must be bored silly with attic games."

"You mean—go out?" Peter asked. "In this?" He sounded as if he were expressing astonishment with all of Scotland. "A complicated country," was what their father kept calling it. In America such a rain would have canceled baseball games and sent Peter and his friends scurrying gratefully to the mall.

"Och, aye." Gran's round face beamed at him. "No one ever melted in this sort of rain."

"We can take Da's big umbrellas," Molly said brightly. "They'll cover us all the way up." She was right. The umbrellas were huge, as tall as Molly. Though at four she wasn't that big.

"And," Gran added, "for all the way down, I think I can find extra wellies."

"Wellies?" Jennifer asked.

"For yer feet, child," Gran explained. "In the wardrobe cupboard."

Without further discussion, Gran sorted out the rain gear in the wardrobe cupboard, which turned out to be the standing wooden closet in the hall.

She handed them each a pair of bright red rubber boots and one each of the enormous golf umbrellas. "The dishes can wait. Or Da can do them, should he get home before us. Though I shall be shocked indeed if he does!" She laughed out loud, as if she had made a great joke.

Jennifer and Molly put on the wellies they were handed, and Molly tromped up and down the entryway happily. Even dry, the wellies made a squishy sound. Frankly, Jennifer thought her wellies were silly looking, but at least they'd keep her feet from getting soaked.

"What about you, Gran?" Jennifer asked.

Tying a flowered scarf over her head, Gran said, "I've lived in this sort of rain since I were a wee lass. Besides, we're not going far. Just down the road."

"You two look like...nerds," Peter said, refusing the red boots.

Jennifer felt the word like a sword in her heart.

"Besides, my Nikes are waterproof." He took his umbrella with barely concealed disdain and opened it while they were still inside the house. FAIRBURN GOLF CLUB was emblazoned in yellow letters on the side.

"Och, bad luck, that," said Gran. "Opening a brolly indoors. Shut it at once, Peter."

Given that Gran knew a thing or two about luck—and magic, as they had already learned in the first days of their visit—Peter quickly drew the umbrella back down, catching his finger in the mechanism and pinching it fiercely. He refused to cry out, of course. At thirteen it would have taken the amputation of a major limb to make him do that.

But Jennifer saw Peter's eyes narrow and knew what that meant. A moment later, when he popped the finger into his mouth like a cork in a bottle, she guessed that it had really hurt. Her own fingertip ached in sympathy. Twins were like that. Where one hurt, the other felt the pain.

So, she thought, *there's the bad luck, then. The finger pinch.*

And the rain.

But, though Jennifer was not to know till later, it was only the start of the luck—some good, some bad, and some terrible.

Two

Eventide Home

As they opened the door a slender, long-haired dog the color of ash pushed Peter aside. Its slim tail beat against his leg.

"Ye daft beings," the dog said, "yer not going on a walk wi'oot me. It's been days since I've had a proper run. The garden's too wee a place for a dog of my size."

Peter looked down. "And let you babble all over town? Not on your life."

Gran smiled. "Only someone who holds magic will be able to understand him. Let the puir fool come along."

"I'll get the leash," Molly said, disappearing back into the house.

"I need no leash, thank ye very much," the dog said. "A word of warning will do if I miss anything. And I *never* miss anything."

"It's the law . . ." Jennifer began.

"In yer land, perhaps," said the dog. "Not in mine."

But by then Molly was back, holding the black plastic collar and leash that their mother had gotten the day after the dog had come to live with them. Not metal. Gran had warned specifically about that: Magic creatures cannot abide metal.

"Here," Molly said, bending to slip it over the dog's head.

And the dog, with little grace, bowed its head to the inevitable, its tail drooping. "I'll wear it for ye, lass, but I dinna have to like it."

■ ■ ■

They went outside then, and walked down the lane, leaving behind Gran's cottage with its grey slate roof that slumped like a farmer's hat. The rain pattered down on the umbrellas, sounding like a code, which Jennifer tried to decipher.

"Is it a message, Gran?" she asked.

"Och, lass, it's just a bit of rain," the old woman answered.

"I was hoping for more magic," Jennifer said. "Like the stuff we had when we first got here. The game of Patience, the wizard's map, the unicorn, the dragon..."

"Ye have that greetin teenie of a dog," Gran pointed out, "for all the use he is."

The dog made a rude noise, somewhere in between a belch and a fart, and Peter giggled.

"And we've got Devil in the garden," Molly said.

Gran nodded. "Yes—the wizard's old black horse. Though we must give him a different name, and soon, I expect. Names are important, you know. Best not be asking for more magic just now."

"Why?" Jennifer hated the bit of whine that crept into her voice. "Why not now? Once we're back in America, I bet there'll be no more magic."

"You don't need magic in a land where everything is electric," Gran told her.

"Well, everything is electric here, too," Jennifer said. "Even the kettle."

"There's electric—and there's power." Gran's voice was adamant. "America's got the electricity and Scotland has the power."

"Then I want *more* of that power," Jennifer said stubbornly.

"Hush, child!" There was steel in Gran's caution. "Never wish for that. Power corrupts."

"Remember Michael Scot," the dog said suddenly, his voice hollow. And for a moment they all walked the lane in silence, remembering the awful wizard who had stolen Molly away and nearly taken over Fairburn a day and a half ago.

"Just for fun, then," Jennifer said at last, trying to salvage something from the conversation.

But Gran's face had lost its softness. "Magic is not something to joke about. Or play with. It is never *just for fun*. Magic is a force that comes when it will. And stays where it will. Few can bid it safely. Beware of folk who joke about magic."

"But *you* can bid it, Gran," Molly said. "You're a witch. And Jen is, too."

"Being a witch and bidding magic to dance are not necessarily the same," Gran said. "Besides, I am a white witch and I deal in herbals. If Jennifer has any true magic, we dinna ken its real source yet. Untrained is untried, as we say. I expect any magic Jennifer has will be touched by her twinship and tinged with American know-it-all. And what that latter be, I canna say, for I hae never been across the lang water."

They continued up the lane.

Peter had a funny, almost angry look that altered his normally pleasant face. Jennifer wondered what was bothering him but was astonished when he blurted out, "I don't see why Jen is the only one with magic when we're twins!"

The dog growled low in his throat, as if agreeing.

Jennifer turned to Peter quickly, using that soothing voice she'd come to rely on lately. "We don't know that I have any magic, really, Peter. And remember what they said in health class—that girls mature earlier than boys. Maybe your magic will be coming later."

He looked away from her and sped up till he was several steps ahead.

"Peter is maaaad," Molly started to chant. "Peter is maaaad."

The dog snapped out, "Little tongues, big wounds," then trotted ahead to Peter's side.

"You may be right, Jennifer," Gran said. "But he is nae ready to hear such wisdom. So let it lie, lass. Let it lie."

Jennifer bit her lip. The one thing she didn't want to do was fight with Peter. A twin fight was always devastating. It hurt worse than anything. She hurried to catch up with Peter. Gran and Molly came right after.

"Remember what I told ye several days ago about magic," Gran said, ignoring Peter's long face. "Here in Scotland, the Major Arcana consist of earth magic, air magic, fire magic, and water magic. The Minor magics are colors, numbers, and riddles. White magic is the proper use of the gift, and black magic is done by the wicked. And Tartan magic is—"

"—old woman's blether," muttered the dog.

"You can say that again!" Peter agreed. He grabbed the leash from Molly, and side by side the dog and boy ran up ahead. Whatever else Gran had to say about magic after that was lost to them.

■ ■ ■

At the end of the lane Peter stopped suddenly, pulling the dog up short as a car whizzed down the cobbled road on the left side.

"Oof!" Peter breathed. "I always forget which way to look. I'm still thinking cars drive on the right, like in America."

"Ye great gomeril," the dog said. "Don't yank my neck aboot."

"Call me another name," Peter said, "and I'll do more than that. I'll—" But as he could not come up with anything horrible enough, he ran his hand through his lank brown hair as if that were some kind of response.

The dog sat down on its haunches, pink tongue lalloping from its mouth, and stared fiercely and silently at him.

"So what's a *gomeril*?" Peter asked at last.

"Ye dinna want to ken that." The tongue slipped back into the dog's mouth, as if it had a mind of its own.

"Oh, but I do."

"A loud-talking fool is what it is. And what ye are, too," said the dog, now scratching behind its right ear with its hind leg.

"Ah," Peter said, then shut up, as much because the others had caught up to them as in reaction to the name the dog had called him.

"Turn left here," Gran said, "and then ahead toward Fairburn."

"How far?" asked Molly.

"A hundred steps," said Gran. "Can you count that high?"

"I'm four," Molly said sternly.

"Then of course you can." Gran smiled. "Start now."

"One, two, three..." Molly began.

They went along the cobbled Double Dykes Road and then up Burial Brae, passing a little cemetery where ancient stones leaned at odd angles. All the while Molly counted aloud— "thirty-six, thirty-seven..."—and the rain kept up its own count on the tops of their umbrellas.

"Dreech," Jennifer whispered. But only because she had come to like the sound of the word.

"Sixty-four, sixty-five..."

On their left a high grey stone wall snaked along the road. Occasional yellow flowers poked through chinks.

"Wallflowers," Gran said, pointing to the little blossoms.

Molly ran her fingers across the stones. "Ninety-seven, ninety-eight, ninety-nine," she said, quite pleased with herself, having really only just mastered the long count.

At "One hundred!" they came to a gap in the wall. Set into the gap was an ironwork gate with intricate Celtic knotwork designs.

"It *is* a hundred, Gran. It *is* exactly! Number magic!" Molly cried.

"Nae magic, child. Except that yer fair young to count so far," Gran said.

Molly made a face, and her bottom lip began to stick out. Jennifer added quickly, "I couldn't count that far till I was five."

The tantrum was averted and Molly's sunny disposition returned. She pointed to a plaque, quite mossed over and a bit difficult to make out. Standing on tip-toe, she spelled out the words. She did not get them all right, but enough. Jennifer helped.

THE MCGREGOR HOSPITAL
FOUNDED AS AN EVENTIDE HOME
BY WILLIAM MCGREGOR
OF PITTENWEEM 1882

"Eventide Home!" Molly clapped her hands. "This is it!"

"This is it, indeed," Gran said.

"But, Gran," Jennifer said, looking through the

gate and into the window of the great stone house, where she could see an old woman in a wheelchair staring out at the rain. "Gran—it's a nursing home."

"Not exactly," Gran said. "The residents here must be able to cope on their own without full-time nursing. It's what we call a registered home for the elderly."

"Elderly? Like you, Gran?" Molly asked.

Gran laughed. "Not exactly."

"*Older* than you?" Molly's voice held something like astonishment.

Gran laughed again. "Much older. And much less able."

"But *Eventide*..." Jennifer mused. "I thought it sounded like something magical."

Gran smiled. "You never can tell." Then she pushed through the gate and walked up the path.

Molly skipped along beside her, curls bouncing, and Jennifer trailed behind. Peter and the dog hung back.

Once at the front door, Gran, Jennifer, and Molly walked up the ramp and disappeared inside.

"Old people," Peter said with a shiver to the dog. "I dunno. Old gives me the jeebers."

"Consider the alternative," the dog told him.

Casting a quick glance to the side of the house, where he could see the tops of some gravestones, Peter nodded in sudden solemn agreement. Not to be left out in the rain, he walked quickly to the stone house and up the stone steps, hauling the dog with him.

Weird Sisters

A young woman in a plaid skirt, white blouse, and blue cardigan sweater greeted them at the door. She had a foxlike face, long and sly looking. A metallic name badge on her collar identified her as Fiona, and she wore a pair of tiny silver scissors around her neck on a ribbon.

"Hello—Mrs. Douglas, isn't it? Have you come to see the girls?" She spoke only to Gran, ignoring the children and the dog entirely.

"I though you said they were *old* people," Molly piped up. "Not girls."

Fiona laughed—a yippy sort of sound—and only then deigned to look down at Molly, as if just noticing her. "A little American, I see."

Gran made a *tsk*ing sound with her tongue and Fiona stopped laughing, but a smile still played around her mouth.

"The girls are in the Garden Parlor," Fiona said. "Though heaven knows why. On such a day I'd rather be nearer the fire myself."

She took the wet umbrellas and put them in a ceramic umbrella stand.

"Follow me," she said to Gran, once again acting as if the children and the dog did not exist. Then she led them through two sitting rooms crowded with heavy stuffed chairs and sofas upholstered in floral prints. Ugly wooden floor lamps with knotted-fringed shades sat beside each chair, while wooden end tables butted up against the sofas.

In the first parlor a few old women sat on a sofa, chatting in a language Jennifer could not understand. In the second a bald man in a wheelchair, fringed lap robe over his legs, dozed by a fire, his breath spurting out noisily. The old woman Jennifer had seen through the window was also in the second parlor, still staring out at the gate. She had a crocheted shawl over her shoulders and a peculiar lacy cap, like a baby's bonnet, on her head.

"Did you magic the lady, Gran?" whispered Molly. "Is that why she stopped laughing at me?"

She tried to make the same *tsk*ing sound and failed.

"I shamed her," Gran whispered back. "For some it comes to the same thing."

There was a smell in the rooms that Jennifer could not put a name to, a kind of musty, flowery, lemon-and-pine-sachet smell. But beneath that odor was something darker and heavier, something uncomfortable and edgy, something that made Jennifer's throat ache as if she had strep. She wondered if that darker, heavier smell was old age. Except Gran didn't smell like that. Or Da.

And then they were in what could only be the Garden Parlor. It was an all-over-glass room full of green and flowering plants sitting in heavy ceramic jardinieres. Rain pattered away on the glass roof and against the windows. The chairs here were wrought iron, painted white, with cushions covered in tartan plaids. Little lace doilies, looking terribly out of place, lay over the back cushions.

Three old women—each clearly much older than Gran, though none of them had hair quite as white as hers—were playing cards around a glass-topped table. One had set out the pattern and the other two were busy commenting on it. A fourth chair at the table stood empty. Teacups were at each place and a tea service—pot and creamer and sugar bowl—waited on a small table nearby. The three were so engaged in their game that they didn't notice that visitors had come in.

"It's Patience!" Peter said, the first words he'd spoken since entering the Eventide Home. "Look, Jennifer, they're playing Patience."

His voice was surprisingly loud in the glass room, and the three old women looked up slowly.

"An American! And a boy!" said one, a lady with pink-tinted glasses pinching her sharp nose and a face like a dried-up apple.

"Canna be American if he kens the game," said the second. "There's nain in America still kens it." She was round and soft, and looked as if she were as upholstered as the parlor chairs.

But the third, imperious as a queen, with hair dyed an improbable shade of orange, threw down the cards. "Here at long last, Gwennie," she said loudly. "And what has taken ye so long? The place is dull and boring wi'oot ye!"

"The girls," Fiona said unnecessarily, and fled the room.

Sniffing loudly, the dog walked stiff-legged over to one of the windows, where he gazed out longingly. Peter joined him there and they stood silently, hip to shoulder, staring out at the sodden garden as if it were their only hope of escaping the awful regiment of women.

"Dinna be afraid, dearie," the soft woman called to Molly, who, suddenly overcome with shyness, had hidden behind Gran. "Come and let me see ye."

Molly refused to budge.

But Jennifer threw caution to the winds. "Are you all part of Gran's coven?" She knew that witches gathered in covens.

"Do ye mean, are we Weird Sisters? Hags? Crones?" asked the pinched-faced one.

"Carlines?" added the soft one. "Cummers?"

"All of the above!" declared the orange-haired old lady happily. "But in this day and time, so as not to disturb the populace, we call ourselves a sewing circle. After all"—and she winked heavily at Jennifer, a long, slow lowering of the left eyelid—"they burned witches here in Fairburn up through the middle of the nineteenth century."

The dog whispered to Peter, "Sewing circle, my left hind leg!"

"Maybe they should call it a *spelling* bee!" Peter whispered back.

"Spelling bee!" The dog shouted with laughter.

"It talks!" the orange-haired weird sister cried. "Gwennie, how did ye? Where did ye?"

"When did ye?" asked the other two.

"Not I," Gran said. "Not at all. It were these three found him. My granddaughter's bairns. And Americans, as ye have observed. There is some magic across the water, though neither they nor we ken what it is yet."

Jennifer explained carefully that Gran and Da weren't *exactly* her mother's grandparents. They were older cousins who had taken care of Mom's mother during the war, when all the rest of the family had perished in one way or another—parents in the buzz bombs in London, real grandparents in a train trying to escape afterward.

"Kin is kin and clan is clan," pronounced Gran. "And these three"—she pointed to the card players—"are my friends, but the four of us are as close as sisters."

The three old women each raised a teacup at that.

"To friendship," said the orange-haired one. And they all drank.

After that, of course, there were introductions all around, as the old ladies peppered the children with questions about where they were staying and for how long they planned to visit and the like.

The soft, round lady was Mrs. Campbell; the pinched-faced one was Mrs. McGregor.

"Like the man on the plaque!" Molly cried, coming from behind Gran at last and clapping her hands. "Mr. McGregor's Eventide Home."

"What a lovely child!" said Mrs. McGregor. "And so bricht."

"Oh!" Molly said.

"What is it, child?"

"And there's Farmer McGregor in *Peter Rabbit*! Peter ate all his lettuces."

The old ladies beamed at her.

Peter muttered down to the dog. "And Rob Roy was a McGregor, too. I saw the movie. So what?"

Everyone ignored him, including the dog.

"Well—I am Maggie MacAlpin," said the orange-haired lady. She looked very serious. "It is very special that I tell ye my true name, ye ken that? Not just my married name, which is Maggie

MacAlpin Morrison. But Morrison being long dead, I've gone back to my own name."

Jennifer remembered Gran mentioning the power of names. And she remembered, too, that in one of the fantasy books she loved—it might have been *A Wizard of Earthsea*—the author spoke of the importance of naming. She kept her mouth shut, to keep from asking the impolite question.

But Molly—with the innocence of a preschooler—had no such qualms. "Is Maggie your whole name? Or is it just some of it? My *whole* name is Molly Isabelle—"

"Molly!" Jennifer said, almost as a warning.

Maggie MacAlpin threw her flame-colored head back and roared with laughter. Then she leaned over and gathered Molly up, letting her sit on the glass-topped table.

"Here ye go, Molly Isabelle," she said. "Tell us more about yerself."

It all seemed terrifically friendly, but Jennifer noticed that Maggie MacAlpin had never actually answered Molly's question. And by putting Molly on the table, she had also destroyed the pattern of the Patience game.

Talisman

Jennifer started toward her sister protectively, but Gran stopped her, putting a hand out.

"Nothing to fear, Jennifer. They like bairns—children, that is."

"Probably like to eat them for dinner," Peter muttered. He and the dog walked out of the Garden Parlor together, heading toward the inner rooms and—Jennifer presumed—the door outside.

She longed to follow them and take Molly with her.

But Molly seemed to be enjoying herself. She was actually flirting with the old ladies, or at least trying to charm them, which in Jennifer's opinion was one and the same.

"Gran . . ." Jennifer began, the whine back in her voice. She had a sudden sharp, icy pang of fear, like a cold hand on her back, which she couldn't explain. For a moment the room seemed to darken, as if the lights had dimmed. Jennifer blinked and everything was right again.

But Gran had joined her friends at the table, sitting in the empty chair and chatting away in a sprightly combination of English and Scots that left Jennifer feeling grumpy and left out.

Redheaded Maggie MacAlpin must have sensed Jennifer's unhappiness, for she suddenly turned. Looking right at Jennifer, she said:

> *Hokey pokey, a penny the lump,*
> *The more ye eat, the more ye jump.*

Jump Jennifer certainly did, afraid that Maggie MacAlpin had just set some sort of spell on her. She put her hands up as if to ward off something invisible.

"Well?" asked Maggie MacAlpin. She was grinning in a way that Jennifer felt was directed *at* her.

Jennifer wriggled her fingers but at last had to admit she did not feel enchanted, did not feel trapped in any kind of sorcery at all—not like the other day, when the wizard Michael Scot had spoken a spell and the air had simply hummed with magic.

"Well?" Maggie MacAlpin asked again. "Do ye in fact want some?"

Gran laughed. "She's no idea what ye mean, Maggie. They have nae such a verse in America, I'm guessing."

"Nae such a verse? And what is the world coming to if a child dinna ken those words? I mean *ice cream,* child," Maggie MacAlpin explained. "That's how my own granny used to ask me if I wanted any. Would ye like some? Ice cream cold enough to make ye jump."

"On a cold, rainy day like this?" Jennifer's voice was full of scorn. *"Dreech!"*

"Och, they've nae manners, these Americans," said Mrs. McGregor.

"Yes, please," said Molly.

With that, the three old ladies turned their attention back to Molly, which Jennifer found to be a kind of relief. But then they went on and on about how lovely Molly was, and what good manners she had, and what pretty dark curls she had. It got pretty sickening.

At that very moment, in came Fiona carrying a bowl and spoon, some hand-knit tasseled shawls over her arm. "I thought the wee one might like some ice cream. It's vanilla and chocolate mint swirl. A favorite, I am told, among American children."

"The very best," said Maggie MacAlpin, taking the bowl from her and giving it to Molly.

Fiona looked out the window at the rain and, shaking her head, placed a shawl over the shoulders of each of the old women. "Now, ladies," she said softly, "can't have you getting a chill."

There was a small protest from each of them, but the shawls were draped nonetheless, and Fiona turned to Gran. "Best you have one, too, Mrs. Douglas, or ye'll be living here sooner than ye think."

"I'm not cold in the least, thank you very much," Gran snapped. "And if it be dreech, it's but a wee bit o' dreech. I hae lived in it my whole life long."

Looking put out, Fiona set the extra shawl down. She poured fresh tea into the teacups, and then she was gone, back into the main part of the house.

Back, Jennifer thought, *to stand near the fire. I wish I were with her.* She shivered. With cold this time, not fear. *I could use that shawl!* But she didn't ask, fearing Gran's ridicule. Or her friends'.

"How is it, dearie?" Mrs. Campbell was saying to Molly, whose face was already a smear of ice cream.

Jennifer was not amused. She knew with sudden and irritating certainty that the three old ladies—and probably Gran, too, for that matter—had arranged that little display of Minor magic for her sake. How else to explain Fiona coming in with just the one bowl, and right on cue? The fact that Molly got to eat something delicious and that Jennifer didn't was entirely beside the point.

I hope it is *cold enough to make her stomach jump,* thought Jennifer grimly.

"I have something," said Mrs. McGregor, in a small, muzzy voice. "For the curly-head. A talisman. I found it...weeding...the graves..." Her voice trailed off, as if speaking had suddenly become an effort.

"What's a tallyman?" asked Molly.

Oh no, Jennifer thought, starting to turn away. *It's too much. I should* have gone to stand by the fire *with Fiona. Or out with Peter and the dog.* But she didn't turn quickly enough. Out of the corner of her eye she saw Mrs. McGregor hand Molly what looked like a painted stone about the size of a fifty-cent piece.

"Ooooo," Molly said, clutching the stone.

"Taken!" said Maggie MacAlpin mysteriously. "Taken!" But she also sounded weak, as if she were about to faint. Then suddenly she sat up straight, adding, "Waken. Mistaken. Shaken."

Gran looked at her with sharp curiosity. "Maggie, what are ye havering about?"

Maggie MacAlpin didn't respond directly. Instead she made one more effort at rousing herself, and glared at Molly. "Give it me!"

But Molly pouted, clutching the stone talisman to her chest. "Mine," she said, just as Maggie MacAlpin fell asleep in the middle of reaching for the stone.

Both Mrs. McGregor and Mrs. Campbell began to doze, too, their chins resting on their chests.

Jennifer knew that nursing homes often over-medicated their patients. She'd seen a TV special on the problem and written a paper for her American Civics class called "Where the Old Folks

Go." (Got an A-plus, too, while Peter's paper on drugs and the Olympics had only gotten an A-minus, which was surprising.) So Jennifer guessed that all three of the Eventide ladies were probably on pills, like Valium or some other kind of tranquilizer.

She shivered, recognizing the fear sensation again. *A kind of feeling of darkness,* she thought, though this time the lights stayed on. The heavy smell of old age only seemed stronger now that all three of the women were asleep, Maggie MacAlpin snoring with her mouth wide open.

Jennifer knew with sudden certainty that she had to get some fresh air.

■ ■ ■

She found Peter and the dog standing on the front steps, staring out at the bucketing-down rain. They both looked miserable.

"Umbrella full of holes?" she asked. "Or afraid of melting?"

Peter gestured at the dog. "He refuses to move."

"I'm waiting for a drier day," the dog said.

"You'll be here till next summer, then," said Peter ferociously, handing the leash to Jennifer.

"You take charge of him. The two of you are quite a pair! I'm going off on my own." And away he went, umbrella raised high.

"Peter!" Jennifer called after him, but he didn't even turn to look back. Once he was through the gate, the high stone walls hid him from view, though she did catch a glimpse of the umbrella as it moved along the road.

"Now look what you've done," said Jennifer, turning to the dog. "He's as upset as I've ever seen him."

"Done? Done? I've done nothing but what I should. You're the one who challenged him. I'm only guarding the wee lass."

"Out here?"

"Better than in there," said the dog. "That place reeks of darkness."

"I sensed something, too," Jennifer said, trying to salvage something with the dog. "And for a moment I thought the lights had gone out...Gran says you don't have the kind of electricity we have in the States. So maybe the Eventide Home needs a better generator or something."

"Humans have nae noses," said the dog. "It's a shame, but there it is. The worst of the reek, though, surrounds those three auld carlines."

"Is it old age?" Jennifer asked.

"Only a bairn would ask that," muttered the dog.

"But those are Gran's friends," Jennifer said, trying not to remember how uncomfortable their drugged sleep had made her just moments before. "And they must be *good* witches—*white* witches—because Gran is."

"Who kens yer weaknesses better than a friend?" the dog asked her, adding, "Or a twin. And as for good or bad, dark or light, the nose never lies."

Just then the door opened behind them, and Gran and Molly came out holding the umbrellas.

"Look, Jen!" Molly said, traces of ice cream still on her lips. "Look, what Mrs. McGregor gave me before she fell asleep."

This time Jennifer looked closely. The little rock wasn't painted at all, but rather engraved with a strange picture of a bird on top of a snake. The thing almost seemed to glow.

"It's a tallyman. Isn't it pretty?"

"*Talisman*," Jennifer corrected her. *Pretty* was not what she would have called the stone. Spooky, perhaps. Scary, maybe. Dangerous, definitely.

Lost Stone

Where's Peter?" asked Gran.

"He's gone on home," said Jennifer, careful not to mention their fight.

"Nae that way," the dog said. "The gormless lad went left who should have gone right."

"Is Peter lost?" asked Molly, looking terribly worried.

"Not so much lost as bothered," Gran assured her. "It is very difficult to get lost for long in a town as small as Fairburn. He'll get home soon enough. And so should we." She looked up and smiled. "The rain is over for now." Then, taking Molly by the hand, she headed determinedly toward the gate, the dog trotting by her side.

Umbrella tightly furled, Jennifer hurried after them.

They turned right on Burial Brae, onto the

cobblestones, and Molly pulled her hand from Gran's. She skipped ahead on the sidewalk, throwing her stone talisman straight up into the air and catching it two times out of the first three throws.

"Be careful, child," Gran called out as a car passed by on the cobbled road. Molly was scrabbling at the curb for her little stone after the one missed throw.

But whether Molly heard Gran and ignored her or simply misunderstood was not clear, for she threw the talisman up again and this time it went too high, hitting a tree branch and ricocheting over the stone wall into the cemetery.

For a stunned moment no one said anything. Then Molly wailed. "My tallyman!"

"*Talisman*," Jennifer muttered through clenched teeth.

Gran said, "Guide us!" fervently.

And the dog sat on his hind end and howled.

"Gran, Gran," Molly cried, running back to them. "Do something. Mrs. McGregor gave it to me. I can't lose it. I can't." She was close to hysterics.

"Oh, for goodness' sakes," Jennifer said, "it's just a stupid stone."

"It's a *talisman*," wailed Molly, this time saying it correctly.

"I'm afraid she is right," said Gran. "It would be a terrible thing to lose that stone. I feel that in my bones. Will ye go in and look for it, Jennifer, dear? The gate's by the side there."

"In the *cemetery*?" Jennifer didn't know why that should so appall her. There was a cemetery called Willowbrook near their home in Connecticut, and she and her friends played in it all the time. But this cemetery was centuries older than the one back home, and something just felt strange about it. She had that same feeling of foreboding she'd had inside the Eventide Home. Only stronger. She wished Peter hadn't left. She needed him. He was always braver about things than she was.

"Go," Gran said. "Now. I have my hands full here." And indeed she did, with Molly and the dog making equal rackets.

So Jennifer looked where Gran was pointing.

Down a tiny lane that was much too narrow for a car, she saw a small ironwork gate. Taking a deep breath, she gave Gran her umbrella and went along till she reached the gate. Then she pushed on it with both hands.

It made an awful creaking noise, like something out of a bad horror movie, but moved less than an inch. She wondered if it had been opened in years. But then, when she pushed on it again, shoving with her shoulder, it opened slowly, protesting all the way.

She went in.

There was a kind of hushed reverence inside the cemetery, made more intense by the fact that both Molly and the dog had suddenly and without explanation fallen silent beyond the wall.

The cemetery was small, about the size of their backyard at home, and easily contained within the high stone walls. There was another ironwork gate on the other side, which led to the Eventide Home's lawn. Jennifer could see a patch of green.

The grass inside the cemetery had recently been cut and rolled flat. However, the forty or so gravestones were not so well tended. They seemed ancient, the inscriptions on them mostly obscured by moss or rubbed flat by the passing years. Jennifer could hardly read a word or date on each: "Drowned...1745...lost at sea...invictus...1567... salvation..." None of the stones stood up straight. They leaned like drunken old men.

Jennifer went over to the wall that paralleled Burial Brae Road. A huge oak shaded the area, and several of its limbs overhung the wall. The corner was dark—much too dark for the time of day— and she looked around.

A sea mist—which Gran called a haar—had come in sudden and thick and fast and was flowing over the wall. It was an odd grey, the color of stew left three days in the pot.

The silence that Jennifer had noticed was suddenly muddied by a muffled roar, like a radio broadcast of a battle, not quite tuned in. She thought she heard faraway shouts, cries, and she turned around to see where the sound was coming from. But she was all alone in the grey mist in the graveyard.

She kicked at the sparse vegetation under the oak with her wellies—and suddenly her foot must have connected with the little stone, for it skipped across some long slabs of rock that were laid out inside shallow depressions like four open graves beneath the tree. At that very moment the mist lifted and the radio was turned off.

She chased after the talisman and found it lying—incised side down—in the smallest of the open depressions, which looked about the right size for a child to be buried in.

When she picked up the stone she heard a voice gabbling at her in an unknown language. Looking up, she saw a girl not much taller than Molly but clearly twice Molly's age.

Sun browned and black haired, dark eyed and wiry, the girl had on a scraped leather skirt like Native Americans once wore. Jennifer had studied Native Americans in school, not once but many times, and this girl had the haunted, hunted look of some of the tribal photographs in the textbooks. Instead of a shirt or blouse, the girl had on a woven cloak held together in the front by a large silver brooch. Jennifer had seen that same kind of pin in the tourist shops on Fairburn's High Street.

The oddest thing about the girl, though, was that her hands and arms were covered with blue tattoos. *Real tattoos,* Jennifer thought, *not the paste-on, wash-off type*. Not so odd, perhaps, if the dark girl had been a teenager, some sort of runaway, living rough on the streets. But she didn't look as if she were any older than seven or eight, and surely that wasn't allowed—not in America and not in Scotland, either.

She had not an ounce of fat on her, either. *As if,* Jennifer thought suddenly, *she was only an ounce away from starving.*

The girl stood imperiously, hands on her hips, still speaking in her strange tongue.

"You frightened me!" Jennifer said, but in a joking way. "I didn't see you come in."

The girl was obviously in no mood for jokes. She held her hand out toward Jennifer and gestured at the talisman. Then she spoke a quick, sharp command. Jennifer didn't know the words, but it was clear what the girl meant.

Give me the stone.

Six

Lost Child

A howl made them both turn around. The dog was sitting at the gate but would not come in.

"Dark!" he was howling. "Dark!"

Gran pushed past him, holding Molly by the hand. "Have ye got it?" she said, coming to stand next to Jennifer. "Have ye found the blessed thing?"

The dog continued to howl.

"I want my talisman," Molly cried.

"So does she," said Jennifer, pointing to the dark-haired girl glowering under the tree.

It was as if they hadn't seen the girl until Jennifer pointed her out. Then Molly shut her mouth and Gran's mouth dropped open.

And the dog stopped howling.

The girl repeated the same unintelligible phrase to Gran that she'd said to Jennifer and held out her hand. As she did, the cloak fell away from her arm and Jennifer recognized one of the tattoos.

"Look!" Jennifer said. "Isn't that tattoo the same bird and snake as on Molly's stone?"

"It is indeed," said Gran.

The dark girl repeated her demand.

"Is it the Gaelic, then?" called the dog from behind the gate. He was now pacing back and forth. "Is she speaking the old tongue?"

Gran turned and bade him enter the cemetery, her fingers shaping some kind of warding spell.

The dog came in slowly and reluctantly, making certain that he did not touch any part of the ironwork. His tail hung down between his legs.

When at last he got to Gran's side, she answered him. "Not Gaelic. Not Scots. Not any language I ken. Is it something older, dog?"

The dog sniffed the air, then he shivered all over. "Older than ye think, carline. Older than even I can guess at."

"I thought so," said Gran, nodding her head. "A Pict, by the look of her."

"Don't give her my talisman," wailed Molly. "Mrs. McGregor gave it to *me*."

"What's a Pict?" asked Jennifer.

"One of the oldest races in Scotland," said Gran.

"Is she like . . . like a gypsy?"

"Nothing like," said Gran. "There are still Travelers—gypsies, as ye call them—about in Scotland today."

"Then what's she doing here?"

"That's what I do not ken, Jennifer," said Gran, shaking her head. "There haven't been Picts in Scotland for a thousand years or more."

The Pictish girl had obviously gotten tired of waiting to be given the stone, and she made a rush at Jennifer to take it. But Jennifer was older and—if not quicker than the girl—at least a lot taller. She held the stone high over her head and the girl could not get at it, much as she screamed and spat. She aimed a kick at Jennifer's knee, which—if it had landed—might have done some damage, but Jennifer quickly jumped aside. Her karate lessons hadn't been in vain, then, she thought with satisfaction.

"Mind your manners!" Jennifer told the girl, which was something Mom often said to them.

Suddenly the dog began to howl again. It was a terrible sound, high and keening, that raised the little hairs on the back of Jennifer's neck.

"Dark!" he howled. "Dark, dark, dark."

Gran's simultaneous intake of breath made Jennifer turn around.

Behind her, under the tree, the dark grey haar had returned, and the noise as well. It didn't take a witch—or a rocket scientist—to know that what was forming was not something good.

"Out!" shouted Gran, pointing to the gate they had come in. "Molly, Jennifer—out of this place right now!"

The dog needed no telling. Tail still firmly between his legs, he galloped through the gate.

Jennifer whirled, grabbed Molly by the hand, and raced after him.

Huffing, Gran followed.

"The gate!" Gran said as soon as she had gotten through it. "Pull the gate closed. Cold iron will keep it in—whatever it is. Fey things cannot stand cold iron." She placed both hands on the gate and began to pull.

Jennifer helped and the gate, again protesting with a high squeal, began to swing shut slowly.

At the very last minute, the dark girl slipped past the gate as well, running just ahead of the dark mist. Screaming something none of them could understand, she put her own hands on the gate and pulled along with them.

With one last protesting squeak, the gate closed.

Behind it the dark formless mist swirled but could not get through.

"That was close," said Jennifer.

"*Much* too close," Gran agreed.

But then they heard someone sobbing. Turning, they saw it was the Pictish girl, her hands held up in front of her as if in some kind of supplication.

"Gran, she's burned her hands," cried Molly. "How did she get burned?"

But Jennifer knew without being told, because the burns cutting across the dark girl's hands were the same shape as the bars on the gate.

"Iron," she said to Molly. "Cold iron burned her, but she didn't let go."

"She helped save us all," added Gran grimly. "Blessed be."

Blessed be, indeed, Jennifer thought.

"Can I have my talisman now?" asked Molly, holding out her hand.

Wordlessly Jennifer handed the stone over, her thoughts at that moment not at all charitable toward her little sister.

But then Molly did something that surprised them all.

"Here," she said, "this is really yours." And she handed the talisman to the Pictish girl, who closed her poor, burned right hand over it and held fast.

Seven

The Back End of History

As they walked down the lane, conscious that just beyond the stone wall a dark mist was stalking them, the rain started up again in earnest.

Jennifer snapped open her umbrella.

The Pictish girl gave a little scream and ran out onto the cobbles.

"Come here, child," Gran called. "Or ye'll be run down."

Luckily no car came by while they coaxed her back onto the sidewalk, but she would not walk under either of the umbrellas. Indeed, the very sight of them seemed to send her into a panic. So Gran stayed behind with her while Molly and Jennifer walked on ahead.

As quickly as the rain had begun it ended, and a

fiercely hot sun came out from behind the dark clouds. First Jennifer, then Molly shut their umbrellas, and only then could Gran convince the Pictish girl to close ranks with them.

"Has she never seen an umbrella, Gran?" asked Molly.

"No, my sweet," said Gran. "And what she will make of cars and stone houses and running water and electric lights, I canna begin to guess."

"And the telly? Has she seen a telly before?" Molly asked. She had already picked up more Britishisms than the rest of the family combined, and was using them interchangeably with her American words.

"Of course she hasn't seen a TV before," Jennifer said.

"How can *you* know, Jen?" asked Molly.

"Because TV was invented in this century. And that girl is hundreds of centuries old," Jennifer said.

"She doesn't *look* hundreds of centuries old," said Molly. "Only a little older than me."

"She...her...the girl..." Jennifer shook her

head. "Gran, we can't keep calling her that. Does she have a name, do you suppose? I mean, one that we can pronounce?"

"I dinna ken how to ask her," admitted Gran.

"I do," said Molly. She turned to the dark girl and put her hand on her chest. "Me Molly," she said. Then she touched the girl on the arm. "Who you?" She turned back to Gran, grinning. "I saw that in a movie."

"Me Molly!" the girl said seriously.

"No, no. *Me* Molly!" Molly's face got red. "Not you." She stamped her foot.

The girl put her hand—the one without the talisman—over her mouth. Her dark eyes were full of laughter. When she had control of herself again, she touched Molly's arm. "Me Molly," she said. Then she put her fist, thumb side in, on her own chest. "Ninia."

"Ninia!" Molly crowed. "Her name is Ninia!"

The dog growled, "Or her chest is Ninia. Or her heart. Or—"

"Shut up, dog!" Jennifer said. "If Molly says that's the Pictish girl's name, that's her name."

"Quite right," agreed Gran. "At least that is what we will call her."

■ ■ ■

They walked on to the junction where Burial Brae turned into Double Dykes Road, and—luckily—no cars went by. Gran hurried them along so that they got safely and quickly to Abbot's Close. Gran's house, whitewashed and welcoming, stood but a little way down the lane.

Sitting on the doorstep was Peter, his face as long as a ruler.

"What took you all so long?" he asked. "I didn't have a key." Then, catching sight of Ninia, he added, "Who's she?"

Jennifer tried to explain, and then Gran. Even Molly had a try at it, but Peter just shook his head.

"A Pict? How can she be a Pict? Weren't the Picts all dead hundreds of years ago?"

"Millions," Molly said.

"Exactly," Gran replied.

"Exactly...what?" asked Peter. His lips shut tight, as if locking up his entire face.

"I expect it has to do with the back end of history," Gran said.

"And what's the back end of history?" Peter asked reluctantly.

"What a glundie," said the dog. "Everyone kens that."

"Glundie or not, *I* don't know it," said Peter.

"Me neither," said Jennifer stoutly. Peter was, after all, her twin. And if he was to be a glundie—whatever that was—then so was she.

He looked up at her gratefully.

"The back end of history is the word *story*," said the dog. There was triumph in his voice.

Molly clapped her hands. "A story!" she cried.

"Och—well, only as much of the story as I ken," said Gran, fitting the key to the door and letting them all in. "The encyclopedia will have to fill in the rest. History, unlike story, is untidy with its endings."

They dropped their umbrellas in the metal stand and took off their wet wellies. Peter's Nikes were sopping and so he left them on the welcome mat.

"Give the dog a bowl of water," Gran said. "I will put some unguent on the puir girl's hands. And then I will make us all some iced tea. After, we can sit in the garden and see what we can learn about the Pictish folk."

■ ■ ■

Twenty minutes later, having wiped off the various garden seats and the table with a towel, they sat and drank their sweetened iced tea while Gran told them what she knew of the Picts, supplementing it with an article in the encyclopedia that lay open on her lap.

Ninia did not stay with them. She was too busy exploring—first the house, where Da's tankful of tropical fish fascinated her, then the garden, where the rose arbor caught her eye. But she never got so far away that she did not have them all in her sight.

"Once upon a time," said Gran, "the Picts were the only ones who lived here in Scotland—only it wasn't called Scotland then, but Pictland."

"Pictland," Molly said solemnly.

"Well," Gran admitted, "at least that is what the historians call it now. The de'il only kens what the Picts called it."

"Mayhap they called it Ninia," said the dog. "Mayhap she's a Ninian and not a Pict at all." He circled on the paving stones three times before lying down.

Gran ignored him. "The Picts were to us as the Indians are to ye in America. Brave warrior tribes who lived in Scotland before us. They painted—or tattooed—their skins. The name Pict means just that: 'Painted men.' At least, that is what the Romans called them."

"Like the first American settlers calling the Indians *redskins,*" Peter said.

"But *redskins* is a racist word," Jennifer pointed out. "We're *not* supposed to use it."

Peter frowned at her as if she had just accused him of being a racist. She wanted to reassure him, but when she tried to smile, he looked away. "Is *Pict* the same?" she asked Gran.

"Perhaps," said Gran. "Perhaps not. We just dinna ken enough about the Pictish folk to be certain. They had no written language and there are no Picts left about to tell us."

"Well—what *do* ye ken?" asked the dog, stretching out on his chosen stone to soak up the sun.

"We ken they lived from the fourth century to the ninth," said Gran, tapping her finger on the encylopedia. "That they were ruled by kings but that the line was through the women's side, not the men's. A king's nephew reigned after him—son of his sister, not his own son." She closed the book carefully.

"Weird," said Peter.

"Only to you!" Jennifer nudged him. "Oink!"

"Oink yourself!" Peter said back.

"Still, it *was* a king who ruled," Gran pointed out. "Not a queen."

"Hah!" said Peter. "One for the male side!" He took another big slurp of the iced tea.

Sometimes, Jennifer thought sadly, *Peter and I seem so far apart. Not nearly as close as we once were.*

"What about my talisman?" asked Molly.

"Och, well—the stone." Gran bit her lip and looked over at Ninia for a moment. The girl was now on her belly in the wet grass and sniffing at various herbs in the garden.

"The stone," prompted Jennifer.

"What we mostly ken about the Picts, besides some blether written by churchmen who were busy trying to convert them to Christianity—and succeeding, too, I might add—comes from the strange engraved stones they left. Ye can find these stones all over Scotland."

"Like *my* stone, Gran?"

"Only a great deal larger, Molly, my lass. Most are taller than ye, some taller than Jennifer and Peter. And several as tall as yer father. We've a few in the Fairburn Museum that were found in the Eventide cemetery. Perhaps we should go there and look at them. The earlier stones had these strange drawings on them."

"Like my bird and snake!" Molly cried.

Gran nodded. "The later stones—after the Picts all became Christians—have Celtic crosses on them. But no one kens what those earlier pictures mean. They may be magic symbols or they may be clan names or they may be grocery lists. We dinna ken for certain."

"Grocery lists!" Molly put both her hands over her mouth and giggled.

"Pretty hard to bring that kind of list to the store with you," said Peter. He laughed, too.

"Maybe it's a list of kings," Jennifer mused aloud.

"Perhaps," said Gran. "And perhaps the wee Pictish lass will tell us."

"If that one could tell us a thing," the dog said, sitting up, "she'd ha' done it already."

At that moment Ninia came over. In her fist was a bunch of herbs from the garden. She named them slowly to Gran in her rough tongue.

"Good, good," said Gran, then she named all the herbs back to Ninia, using the English words. "We call this one thyme and this one rosemary. And this one—"

"Catnip!" put in Jennifer.

As if on cue, Gran's little white cat appeared around the corner of the garden table. Ninia took one look, gave a little scream, and—dropping the herbs—ran into the house.

"I feel the same way," said the dog. Then he put his head on his paws and within moments began to snore.

EIGHT

Dark Mist

It took them a good fifteen minutes and three pieces of shortbread—which Ninia ate with a ferocious appetite—to coax her into touching the little cat. But once she'd been convinced to stroke its silky-soft fur with her fingertips—the only parts of her hands not bandaged up by Gran—she began to smile. She picked the cat up in her arms and after that refused to let it go, carrying it everywhere with her.

Surprisingly the little cat let her cart it around, and it took to lying draped over her shoulders like some furry white shawl. She spoke to it continuously, in a lyrical singsong.

"I bet she's never seen a cat before," said Peter.

"We can let her have this one," said Molly.

"Awfully generous with someone else's pet."

Jennifer felt snippy because she'd wanted the cat herself.

Peter understood at once; twins sometimes have an uncanny knack for knowing this sort of thing. Immediately he backed her in his awkward way, as if their other arguments were long forgotten.

"What if Ninia decides she needs the fur for a hat?" he said. "Or wants a midnight snack of kitty on crackers? And"—he snapped his fingers—"there goes Gran's cat."

"Gran's cat," Gran said, "can take care of itself."

And that was that.

■ ■ ■

They had lunch in the garden—sandwiches on homemade bread, big chunks of cheese, crisps, and glasses of fizzy lemonade. Ninia didn't seem to know what to do with the sandwiches until she took them apart and ate what was inside. The glass with the lemonade utterly defeated her. She kept staring into it and turning it upside down, spilling the lemonade everywhere. But she was wild about the crisps and couldn't get enough of them.

"Bet it's the salt," Peter said. "Salt was probably hard to come by back then."

"They lived right by the sea," Jennifer pointed out. "Plenty of salt there."

Gran shrugged. "Crisps are Da's favorite, too."

The dog woke up to the sound of eating and begged—not entirely successfully—for scraps.

They were partway through the meal, Ninia licking the crisps bag without embarrassment, when the great black horse, Devil, trotted over from beyond the wall. He liked to crop the long grass in the wilder part of the garden and rarely strayed closer to the house.

"Am I missing food?" he asked, his words bumping up and down as he trotted toward them.

This time Ninia showed no fear. She leaped up, gabbling long nonsense sentences, and ran over to him. He stopped at once and stood rigidly, while she put both hands on either side of his long face and blew into his nostrils one at a time.

"Never seen a horse afore, either," the dog remarked sarcastically.

Gran smiled. "Of course she has seen horses. There are Pictish stones with horses carved on them in our museum. But..." And she mused a bit, watching the girl and Devil. "She seems to ken *this* one intimately."

"Blow softly in my nose and ye can ken me intimately, too," said the dog.

Gran aimed a cuff at his ear, but missed.

Just then the horse and Ninia came over to them. Giving an expansive gesture with her left hand, Ninia launched into a long and completely unintelligible speech.

"Well..." Gran said to Devil, "and do ye have some information to impart to us?"

"My lady and I were acquainted in the long-ago..." Devil began.

"My *lady*!" Jennifer exploded. "In *that* outfit?"

"*That* outfit was what young girls wore then," Devil replied.

"In the long-ago, you mean?" Jennifer said.

The horse nodded his head up and down. "And *she* was no ordinary girl then. She was to be the mother of the next king."

"She's way too young to be a mother," Peter put in.

"And ye are way too auld to be a fool," said the dog.

"Awfully old," mused Jennifer to the horse, "if you and she lived with the Picts."

"Och," said Gran, "now things may be coming clear. Ninia's been sent here on a mission."

"Or as an escape," Jennifer added.

"Clear as dirt," the dog said.

"He bites his tongue who speaks in haste," said the horse easily.

The Pictish girl gabbled again.

"Och, well, that was certainly instructive." The dog stood and stretched. Then, stiff legged, he walked toward the garden gate. "Someone best let me out," he said. "I'd rather not mess the garden unintentionally."

Peter got up and followed the dog to the fence. Lifting the ironwork latch, he began to open the wooden door. But even before he'd gotten it pushed partway out, the dog was scampering backward, howling hysterically.

"The dark! The dark! The dark!"

And the mist, which had somehow gotten free of the confines of the cemetery and the binding of the ironwork gates, came pouring into the garden with its sounds of war.

NINE

Night for Day

They all managed to get into the house before the mist entirely filled the garden, but only just. The lunch dishes were left scattered on the garden table, the encyclopedia fell to the ground, and two of the chairs were overturned in their flight.

The mist still looked like a haar, only now it was darker and more menacing. It moved like low rain clouds around the house, obscuring the closest objects, even the wisteria that climbed along the house walls.

Relentlessly the mist turned day into night.

"Wow!" said Molly, pressing her nose up to the living-room window and watching as the dark mist changed form. "Look—there's something in it. I think it's a man. No, a horse. No—"

Ninia grabbed her arm and pulled her away. "Me Molly!" she cried. "Me Molly!"

Meanwhile Gran had gone into the cupboard by the kitchen and, moments later, emerged carrying a large grey toolbox.

"Here," she said, handing out ratchets and hammers, screwdrivers and wrenches to the children. "Stick one in front of each window and door. The brass and iron fixtures on the doors and windows should keep the mist out anyway, but better safe than..."

"...sorry." Peter and Jennifer finished her sentence together.

"Very sorry," Peter added. Though he knew it was stupid, he couldn't get rid of the feeling that it was somehow all his fault that the mist had gotten into the garden at all.

Dutifully all of the children—except for Ninia, of course—ran around the house placing the tools and nails by windows and doors. When those were all set out, they used Gran's sterling silverware, teakettle, pots and pans, and old washtub, too. Ninia didn't help, fearing she'd be burned again, though she stuck close to Molly the whole time.

They had just finished on the second floor when Jennifer had a sudden, panicky thought.

"The chimneys!" she shouted as the mist began to scrabble up on the roof. She could hear mourning doves, in panicked flight, leaving their chimney-pot nests.

Desperately the children raced to the fireplaces in each room and scattered the last remaining bits of metal onto the hearthstones. For good measure, Peter placed several portable metal heaters like fire guards in front of each fireplace.

When they were finished they ran back to the living room, where Gran waited with the dog, the cat, and the horse.

"Will it be enough?" Jennifer asked, panting with the effort of securing the house. "Do you think it will be enough, Gran?"

"For now," Gran said. It was not much comfort.

Day was now entirely night, as the dark mist covered window after window, downstairs and upstairs and—

"The actic!" Molly cried. "What if it comes in the actic?" There were lots of windows up there.

"Attic," Jennifer said automatically.

"We've blocked the attic door with carpet tacks

and paper clips and some screwdrivers," said Peter. "They should hold."

Jennifer started to shake again, just as she had in the Eventide Home. "But the iron gate didn't hold the mist in the cemetery," she said. "And that was much thicker iron. And older."

"Ye needn't ha' reminded us o' that!" the dog said miserably. He lay on the rug and put his paws up over his ears.

"I dinna think the mist came through the cemetery gates at all," Gran said. "I think it flowed over the oak tree and down a limb to the other side. Or else someone released it through one of the gates. And then..."

"And then it followed us home?" Jennifer could not stop shaking.

"Like a dog on a trail," said Peter.

"I resent that comparison," said the dog.

"But why did it follow us?" It was Molly's turn to whine.

"That," Gran said, "is always the real question in any magic. *Why.*"

They sat down together in the living room, the lights on everywhere. It said a great deal about their state of fear that Ninia didn't question—even with so much as a look—what must have been a miracle to her glowing in each light fixture. She just clutched the cat and sat huddled between Molly and Jennifer, unable to speak of her terror to anyone but the horse.

"*Why,*" Gran repeated. "That is what we need to figure out first."

"The mist is after the girl?" suggested Peter.

"Or the talisman," said Jennifer.

"Or us," said Molly.

"Or me." The horse spoke from the corner by the garden door with a kind of awful sorrow. "When Michael Scot first took me from my Pictish past, he tore a hole in history. And it seems to have allowed other beings to slip through. Like Ninia. Like the mist."

"The mist isn't a *being,*" said Jennifer sensibly.

"I believe it is the essence of all the beings of a particular time," the horse said.

"That makes absolutely no sense," Peter interjected.

"It makes every bit of sense," Gran said. "That is why the mist is dangerous. If the wrong part of that essence comes loose in the house...or grabs up one of us and thrusts that one through that hole in time..."

"Why noo?" The dog sat up suddenly on his haunches. "Instead of a hundred years ago? Or a thousand?"

"The stone," Jennifer said thoughtfully. "There has to have been some special magic in that Pictish stone..."

"Which Molly let loose by touching," Peter interrupted.

"Or Mrs. McGregor did," said Molly.

"Or you, Jennifer," Peter added.

"Or all three," said Gran. "Three is an important number in magic. And remember—magic cannot be taken, only given."

The dog lay back down and covered his ears with his paws. "Oh, my puir head," he said. "It's all guesswork. And guesswork is nae work, as they say in the Lowlands."

They ignored him.

"Then when Molly *gave* the stone back to Ninia, the original owner..." Jennifer said.

Her musing was cut short by the horse. "What can we do about the mist, boxed up here? I do not want to go back through that hole. To war. To death. I like the green grass of your garden, old woman." He whuffled and shook his head several times, nearly knocking over a floor lamp.

"What we need to do now is to think clearly," Gran said. "Quietly. Properly. Without emotion putting a cloud as dark as that mist over our minds."

"All very well for ye to say," the dog protested, his paws now off his ears. "I'm greetin wi' terror mysel', and I never got to do my business out in the street."

At that Molly started to cry. She was only four years old, after all. It was a high, panicky wail.

Molly's wailing set Ninia off, and the Pictish girl began to sniffle. Then she squeezed the cat till it yowled in protest. When it scratched her, she dropped it in surprise, and it hid under the sofa.

Cat mewed.

Dog howled.

Horse whuffled.

Ninia wept.

And Molly cried, "I want my mommy!"

"*Mommy!*" Jennifer said. "Oh no!"

Peter looked equally appalled. "How will they get home? Mom and Pop. And Da. How will they get through the dark mist and into the house? We have to warn them. We have to—"

"Dinna fash yersel about that," said Gran. "They're not due for hours yet."

And that's when there was a knock at the door: heavy, frantic, and sustained.

Warrior

They must be here early," Peter cried, jumping up from the sofa. "We've got to let them in before the mist gets them."

"No, Peter..." Gran put a hand out to forestall him. "Who knows what else might come in with them, through that tear in history—"

But it was too late. He'd already run out of the living room and was heading toward the front door.

"Peter!" Jennifer shouted, going after him. "It might be a trick of the mist's."

"What if it's not?" he called back. "We can't leave them out there in it. That's much too dangerous." He unbolted the lock and lifted the latch.

"You daft lad!" screamed the dog. "Dinna make a midden out of a mouse hole. Why would they be knocking? Yer mom and pop and Da each have a key!"

But it was too late. Peter had already cracked the door open and a wisp of the fog was creeping painfully over the metal doorstep.

"Mom?" Peter called out tremulously into the grey mist that was rapidly filling the courtyard. "Pop?"

As if to mock him, the fog called the same names back.

At the garden window, Molly cried, "It's gone. The grey stuff's all gone."

But it was not gone, had merely left the garden and was gathering by the open front door, bunched and thick and ready to push in.

Peter slammed the door shut and locked it again, leaning his back against it. Jennifer pushed against the door as well, as if their combined weight was all that was needed to keep the household safe.

"It's all right," Peter called to the others in the living room. "I shut it again in time. No harm done."

No harm? wondered Jennifer.

Even as Peter spoke, the tiny wisp of fog that had made it across the iron barrier began to take form. It shifted and shaped itself before their horrified eyes, growing into a man. Not a tall man—not nearly as tall as Pop, who was six feet—but a man broad at the shoulder, with well-muscled arms, a full dark beard, and long, dark hair combed over to one side and tied up in a ponytail. He was wearing a short leather tunic and soft leather boots. In one hand he held a large ax, and in the other a long-handled spear. Some kind of embossed leather shield was slung across his back on a leather strap.

The warrior was scary enough in the darkened hallway, but when Peter backed away from him and accidentally rubbed against the light switch, turning on the hall light, the man was scarier still.

Like Ninia, he was tattooed on his hands and arms. But he was also tattooed on his body and face, in great swirling designs, like waves. His startled mouth was open and it was a misery of broken teeth. A livid scar ran down his face, from forehead to chin.

Jennifer screamed and Peter tried to run back into the living room, but the warrior quickly blocked his path, bellowing some awful Pictish war cry. So Peter simultaneously gave him a great kick in the shins and ducked under the man's right arm, the arm with the ax.

It was an incredibly brave and incredibly stupid thing to do, and Jennifer shouted encouragement, as if she were cheering Peter on at one of his soccer games.

The warrior turned and started after him, battle-ax held high. In another second the ax would be swung in a downward stroke, and that would be the end of Peter.

Jennifer's cheer turned into a scream.

But Ninia's voice was louder still. She stood and called out something in three short, commanding syllables.

The warrior looked over, spotted her, and fell to his knees in one movement. He laid down his weapons, first the ax and then the spear; put his head in his hands, and—all unaccountably—wept.

ELEVEN

Single Combat

Ninia walked over to the burly warrior and pushed his tattooed hands away from his face. Then she put her own hands under his chin, lifted it, and said something so softly only he could hear.

"If she blows in his nostrils, I may have to honk," said the dog.

"If you are not silent, *I* may have to kill you," said Devil.

"If someone doesn't explain what is happening," Jennifer said, "*I* may have to scream."

Gran held up a hand and they all quieted. "Clearly she recognizes him. King, father, brother, cousin..."

"Actually," the horse said, moving out into the main part of the living room, but taking care not to step on Gran's good carpet, "he is the high king's war councillor."

"And..." Gran said slowly.

"How do you know there is more, old woman?" the horse asked.

"There is always more in history," Gran said. "It is only in a story that much is left out."

"Besides," Peter said to the horse, "she's a witch. And a grandmother. It's an unbeatable combination."

"Ah." The horse nodded. "I shall remember that."

"Dinna make me angry, horse," warned Gran. "You dinna want that."

Devil nodded. "I will tell you all without threats, Grandmother. The man is first among the Pictish warriors. His name is Bridei mac Derlei, named for the great king of the Picts—Bridei mac Bili. But this one is more familiarly known to his clan as Bridei of the Ax and sometimes Bridei of the Long Scar."

Jennifer's right forefinger traced an imitation of that long scar down her own face, from forehead to chin. She wondered what weapon had made it.

At that moment Bridei of the Ax spotted the horse and stood, right hand held out rigid. He babbled in his outlandish tongue. Ninia put her hand on his arm to calm him, but he kept on go-ing. Whatever he was saying, there was certainly a lot of it.

"Now what?" Gran asked. "What have ye left out *this* time, horse?" She raised a hand in warn-ing.

"Only that we are old friends," Devil said, "the Ax and I."

"So ye said about the lass." The dog looked dis-gusted, or perhaps he was amused. It was diffi-cult to tell which, with his long muzzle. "And are ye personally acquainted with the entire Pictish race?"

"Only the southern Picts," the horse said with-out a trace of irony. "They called me Night of Long Thunder." He walked slowly and carefully over to Bridei of the Ax, avoiding a sofa on the left and a chess table on the right. Lowering his head, Devil waited till Bridei put out his hand. Then he nuzzled the man's palm, blowing hotly into it.

"What an embarrassing display," the dog said.

"I think it's sort of sweet," Jennifer told him. "Like his name."

"Aye—ye would." The dog sat down sullenly.

In a single swift and sudden movement, Bridei

threw himself atop the horse. He grabbed up a fistful of Devil's mane in his hand to use as a rein.

Except for a small series of tremors, like waves under the skin, Devil did not move. It was as if he were waiting for some further signal from the man.

"How *noble*," said the dog. He clearly meant the opposite.

Ninia bent down and picked up first the long-handled spear, then the battle-ax. Even though they were heavy weapons, she did not falter but handed them over to Bridei with familiar ease. Then she took the little stone talisman and plaited it into the horse's mane, tying it in with quick, sure knots.

"Elfknots," whispered the dog. "An old magic bound to the wearer."

"Good magic or bad?" asked Jennifer quietly.

"Depends on the magicmaker's intentions," Gran said. "But I imagine Ninia's are all good."

"I *know* Ninia's good," Molly said with perfect four-year-old assurance. "She's my *friend*."

Peter only *humph*ed through his nose, which, Jennifer thought, was not a judgment at all.

Meanwhile Ninia was running her hand down

Devil's nose slowly and saying something to both the warrior and the horse. It sounded to Jennifer a bit like a prayer, for it was low and melodic and urgent.

As Ninia spoke Bridei nodded once or twice, the scar seeming to pulsate as he listened. When she was finished speaking, he pulled Devil's head to the side with a tug of the mane, till he had them both turned around. A quick nudge with his heels, and Bridei urged Devil forward, riding him right over the rug to Gran.

Once in front of Gran, Bridei bowed his head and called out what was clearly a string of instructions. Then he pointed out the window to the garden.

The horse translated, pitching his voice loud enough for them all to hear.

"It is the custom..." he began, then bobbed his head. "Sorry about the rug."

"Never ye mind that rug," Gran told him. "What custom do ye mean? And be quick about it."

"It is the custom," Devil said again. "Single combat between great warriors."

"Wait a minute," Peter said. "I'm not"—he gulped—"not a great warrior. I just do karate for

78 ■ The Pictish Child

fun—not fight with spears and axes. That's movie stuff. Besides, I'm just a kid."

The horse gave a high laugh that was part snort. "If you were a Pictish lad, you'd be well into spears and axes and probably already fought a battle or three by now. But Bridei does not mean you. He is going back into the past, through that rip in time. And I must go with him. I have no choice, you see." He tossed his head, and the stone tied in his mane flashed up and down. "The talisman compels me. Now that Bridei knows the mother of the next king is safe here—and he believes her safe from the Scots king's long reach—he is going back to issue a challenge to single combat. And *that* will decide the outcome of the final battle."

"What final battle?" Gran asked.

"He didn't say."

"Then *ask* him, you muckle ludicrous beast!" the dog cried.

"I cannot," said the horse.

"Canna—or willna?" asked the dog.

"In this instance it is the same thing," said the horse.

"Och!" the dog cried, and turned away.

"In fact," Devil said quietly to the dog's back, "horses do not talk to the Picts, though we can certainly understand them. As you very well know, most of the time animals do not talk to people at all."

"That's one small truth out of ye," said the dog, turning back.

"Yes—it was only Michael Scot's magic that gave me the British tongue. And the British name. As it gave you yours, dog. Of course, my accent is much more cultivated, for I have had a longer time to practice it. And Devil is a better name than Dog." The horse shook his great head.

"I'll cultivate ye, ye silly steed," the dog told him. "I speak good plain Scots, not that primping Lowlands muck." But there was something other than anger in his voice. It trembled a bit, and Jennifer thought he sounded sad.

"Bridei cannot understand what I say any more than Ninia can," Devil said to Gran. "I can only tell you what they speak about, the girl and the Ax. I cannot talk back to them."

Gran patted his head. "It is all right, my friend. You do what you can."

"So be a good lad," the horse called over to

Peter, "and open the garden door. We must ride out to do battle, Bridei and I."

The dog lay down on the rug, gave a convulsive sob, and covered his head with his paws.

"Are you crazy?" Peter asked. "I'm not going to open any more doors."

Jennifer understood at once. It didn't need a twin to know what was on Peter's mind. He had already let in the dark mist twice. He felt guilty and horribly accountable for that. He was not about to let the mist into their lives a third time.

"Wait a minute," Jennifer said. "I may have a better idea."

They gathered around her and she sketched her plan out quickly. It wasn't much of a plan, actually, but it did have the grace of simplicity. Even Peter agreed.

■ ■ ■

So Jennifer, Molly, and Peter returned to the front door, dragging Ninia with them. There they began to talk loudly and jiggle the handle and fool with the lock, as if they were about to open the door.

They could hear an ominous clanking from the

dark mist, where it lurked in the courtyard, waiting for its opportunity like some wild, ravenous
beast.

Craning her neck, Jennifer stared through a
small window in the entryway. She could see the
darkness gathering in all the nooks and niches of
the entryway. It obscured the stone flower troughs
by the side of the house, and even covered the ivy
that climbed on the wall. Sounds of battle cries
rattled against the window like pebbles thrown
from the past, and she jumped back.

"Rattle the handle again," she whispered to
Peter. "I think we may have it fooled. We want it
all here, and no stray wisps in the garden. To give
Bridei and the horse time to get set. And to make
sure none gets into the house through the garden
door."

As Peter worked the latch up and down one last
time, Jennifer tiptoed back to the living room and
called out to Gran, "Go!"

At Jennifer's cry, Gran gave the lock a quick
twist and yanked open the garden door. Then she
stood aside as the horse—with its bulky rider—
pushed past. As they went by, she clapped Devil

on his rear, which made him jerk forward in surprise. Once horse and rider were through the door, Gran slammed the door behind them and locked it fast.

By then the children had raced back to see if she needed any help.

When it was clear that the door was well shut and bolted, Jennifer ran over to the window and looked out.

For a moment the garden was free of the dark mist, and she could see Bridei clearly. He had both spear and ax raised above his head and was holding on to the horse tightly with his thighs. Devil rose onto his back legs and his front feet pawed at the air while Bridei shouted a loud, ululating challenge that could be heard even through the window.

And then the dark mist responded, rolling over the rooftop and down into the garden like doom, covering horse and rider and table and herbal borders and all. It roiled and boiled from one side of the lawn to the other.

Though Jennifer could not see anything now but the mist, she could hear the clanging sounds of sword and battle-ax and the cries of warriors. She could distinguish the low rumble of carts and the skirling of strange pipes.

"Come on, Bridei!" she shouted. "Come on, Night of Long Thunder."

She thought she heard him call back.

The other children and Gran crowded next to her, adding their voices to hers.

The battle seemed to go on forever.

It seemed to end all at once.

And then the mist was gone.

Gone from the garden. Gone from the house. Gone from any window the children looked out.

Gone.

"Bridei..." Ninia whispered. She threw herself onto the sofa and buried her nose in the cat's furry neck.

"Did they win?" asked Jennifer at last. "Did they lose?"

No one could give her a real answer.

Twelve

Car Ride

W e must get into the car and ride over to the
museum," said Gran. "Now!"

"But why?" Peter asked.

"Because the answer to Jennifer's question
about the outcome of the battle may very well be
there. In the museum."

"No," Peter said, "I mean, why should we go by
car? I thought you were big on walking everywhere. The museum's not far. I went past it this
morning when I—went the long way home."

"Ha!" said the dog. "When he was lost, he means."

"We go in the car because it will be fastest. And
safest."

Jennifer understood at once. "Cold iron," she
said. "In the car we'll be surrounded by cold iron."

"Not me, my lass," said the dog. "Nae cold iron
for me."

"Cold aluminum, you mean," Peter said. "And plastic. And steel. Cars aren't made of iron."

"I have a very old car," Gran said.

■ ■ ■

She wasn't kidding. The car was so old it had a fierce-looking grille like a lion's open mouth at the front end, and huge tail fins at the rear.

"Does this thing still run?" Peter asked.

"Da says it does," Gran told them.

"You mean *you* don't know?" Jennifer ran her hand along the metal surface of the car.

"I don't drive," said Gran.

"Then how, you foolish auld besom, are we to get there?" the dog asked.

"Peter can drive," said Molly brightly. "Pop lets him practice in the driveway. Pop says he's a . . . a natural."

But Peter, who had been looking in through the driver's side window, shook his head vigorously. "Not a shift car, I can't. Not on the left side of the road, I can't. Not—"

The dog interrupted. "You wee, sleekit, cowrin, tim'rous—"

"All right," Peter said, as much to shut the dog up as for anything else. "I'll try. Just no more name-calling."

■ ■ ■

They covered the backseat and back floor with blankets and a down duvet, but even then Ninia and the dog had a hard time breathing, both being creatures of magic now totally enclosed in a metal shell.

Trembling and silent, Ninia perched on the backseat as if on some sort of wild and unpredictable steed. She kept her eyes closed tightly and her hands clasped. Her knuckles—the ones that were not bandaged—were white with the effort.

On the other hand, the dog lay on a blanket on the floor with his teeth clamped together, and growled continuously.

Jennifer pushed up the garage door nervously, in case the mist was still around.

But there was not a sign of mist, or rain.

Jennifer ran to get into the backseat, shoving over next to Ninia.

Luckily Da had backed the car into the garage

and all Peter had to do—once he figured out how to start it and get it into first gear—was to let the car drift down the driveway and out onto the lane.

The first real problem they had was when they had to turn into Double Dykes Road. Peter narrowly missed plowing into a passing motorcycle.

The man on the cycle waved his fist at them and called Peter a name.

Frantically Peter hit the brakes and they were all flung forward. Like all cars of that vintage, it had no seat belts.

Molly screamed. Jennifer cursed—something she never did. Gran cried out, "Keep us!"

And the car died.

It took almost five minutes for Peter to get it started again, for he had flooded the engine without knowing it. They sat, anxiously staring out of the windows and wondering if the mist was going to come back, while he tried and tried again to get the thing to turn over. The whole time they were stuck, Ninia jabbered in her foreign tongue and the dog moaned.

But once the engine started up again, *putt-putt*ing with a steady rhythm, Peter did just fine, though he never did get the car out of first gear.

"Ye *are* a natural," Gran said. "There's American magic in those hands, lad."

Peter was concentrating so hard on the road ahead, he almost did not hear the compliment.

So, Jennifer thought, *that's what American magic is. Electricity and cars.*

■ ■ ■

The old car juggered along Double Dykes, into Burial Brae, and then—with Gran shouting, "Right! Right!"—Peter maneuvered them around a traffic circle and down Market Street to the little museum.

Of course, he did not so much park the car as abandon it by the roadside. At which point they all stumbled out, Ninia and the dog being the most careful, so as not to touch any of the metal parts. Then they raced pell-mell into the little museum.

But they needn't have hurried. There was not a sign of the dark mist anywhere.

Thirteen

Museum

The museum was smaller than Jennifer had expected. It was housed in an old fisherman's cottage, with only two low-ceilinged rooms and a small entryway.

"This is *tiny*," Jennifer said.

"Aye—'tis a wee thing. Not much to it," said Gran. "But it's all we've got."

She paid a pound for a family admission fee to a bored-looking woman in a sweater and dark tartan skirt behind the desk. The woman barely looked up from her magazine and so didn't even notice Ninia's odd dress.

"Ye three take that room," Gran said to Molly, Peter, and the dog. "And we will look at this one."

Jennifer took Ninia by the hand and pulled her over to the first display. In a glass case mounted on the wall there were about eight pieces of worked silver jewelry, not too dissimilar from what Ninia wore. One was identified as a silver mount for a blast horn, another as a silver hair pin. The rest were brooches and rings. All of the silver was covered in designs of Celtic knotwork, as well as with dragon heads and lion heads and birds with long, improbable beaks.

The second display consisted of pieces of gritty, coarse pottery in an oatmeal color that Jennifer thought was not very pretty at all.

In the final display case were three largish stones, each about the size of a chair back. The first was covered with the same swirling designs that had decorated Bridei's chest and arms. The second was crowded with animal drawings, mostly of bulls, though there was something that looked like a man on a horse as well. But the third...

Ninia started jabbering again.

"Gran, look!" Jennifer pointed to the third stone, which had a single snake and bird. "It's her sign. Ninia's!"

Gran read the placard below the stone aloud. "'Found at Campbell's farm, south Fairburn, 1957. Considered a Class III stone, period after

A.D. 800. Both the eagle and the snake are thought to be wisdom signs.' "

"If she's so wise," Jennifer groused, "why can't she speak English?" She was embarrassed the moment the complaint had left her mouth.

"Hush!" Gran said. "No need to sound like that silly dog. Besides, the stone gives us a possible date."

"Why should we need one?"

But Gran's answer was interrupted by Ninia, who could not stop gibbering at the stone. She tried to touch it and her hand hit the glass. She tried a second time, only a little too hard, and an alarm went off.

The woman in the sweater and tartan skirt came rushing in. "Here!" she said. "Don't be touching that."

Jennifer dragged Ninia away from the glass and stood in front of her. "I'm sorry," she said. "It won't happen again."

Meanwhile Molly and Peter, with the dog at their heels, came running in at the sound of the alarm.

"Jeez, Jen, what did you guys do?" Peter asked.

"Nothing," Jennifer said. "Ninia was just a little

overexcited. There's a stone here with her...clan pictures on it."

"Snake and bird?" asked Molly.

Jennifer nodded. "Supposed to be wisdom signs. What's in your room?"

"Just photographs," Peter said. "Of old stones."

"Those are *Pictish* stones," the woman said in a voice full of disgust.

"Did ye read what the experts said about them?" asked Gran.

Peter looked surprised. "Were we supposed to?"

"The lass canna read, nor can I," the dog added.

"I can, too, read," Molly said. "Only it was in hard writing."

"She means cursive," Jennifer explained.

But Gran had already gone past the children and into the second room and was bending over, reading the legend under one of the photographs.

"Och—I have been such a fool!" she cried out. Then she straightened and turned to the children. "How could I have forgotten the history?"

The children and the dog rushed over to see what she was talking about. She was standing before a greatly enlarged and grainy photograph of a very ornate stone. "Look!"

They looked, and Ninia was the first to respond. She fell to her knees and began beating her chest with her right fist and keening.

It was an awful sound. Molly put her hands to her ears and so almost missed Jennifer's reading the placard aloud.

" 'Sueno's Stone,' " Jennifer read, " 'which means "Sven's Stone," is the largest Pictish sculptured stone yet discovered. It lies outside of the old Burghead fortress. Twenty feet high, it has nearly one hundred figures carved upon one side, a Celtic cross on the other. It dates from the ninth century.

" 'The stone depicts scenes of fighting and killing. There are bodies of decapitated prisoners depicted as well.' " She shuddered, then went on.

" 'It is thought that the stone commemorates the alleged slaughter of the Pictish nobles in a single treacherous act by the Scottish king Kenneth mac Alpin, who, in A.D. 843, forged together a single nation of Scots and Picts, by the sword.' "

"Well, what is it, Gran?" Peter asked. "What history do you mean?"

But Jennifer knew, even though Peter seemed to have forgotten.

"Kenneth *mac Alpin*," she said.

"That's Maggie's name!" shouted Molly, clapping her hands. "Do you think Kenneth is her daddy?"

The dog laughed, a low, lugubrious sound, almost like a howl. "Her father?" He laughed again. "More like her great-great-great-great-great—" Peter jerked his collar, cutting him off.

"Taken," Jennifer said, suddenly remembering what Maggie MacAlpin had been saying before she fell asleep. "Waken. Mistaken. Shaken."

"Enough!" cried Gran.

"Enough is right," said the woman in the sweater and plaid skirt, coming into the room. "You lot are much too wild for this little museum. I'll be happy to refund your money."

"We were just leaving," Gran told her. "Keep the pound, for all the good it does ye. We have gotten at least a pound's worth of information here."

Gran swept out of the door as if she were royalty, and the children followed her. For a brief moment the dog considered leaving a small token behind, but he thought better of it and galloped out through the closing door.

FOURTEEN

Eventide Again

By the time they all got into the car, it had started to rain, and a steady drumroll sounded on the car's roof. Peter couldn't find the windshield wipers for the longest time, and when he finally did, they made a groaning sound and swiped a great fog across the window.

At first Jennifer thought the dark mist had returned, but gradually the windshield cleared up, and Peter got the car going again. *It isn't,* Jennifer thought, *the least bit like magic.*

Since Peter couldn't figure out how to put the car into reverse, they had to go the long way around, right through the very center of Fairburn. The car moved in short, sharp jerks as Peter tried to avoid the other cars and a horde of pedestrians, all of whom suddenly seemed in league against them.

Everyone inside the car was now shouting advice to Peter all at the same time—even Ninia, though what she was saying no one could guess.

Peter was close to losing his temper or crying, whichever came first. Jennifer recognized the pinched look on his face all too well.

"Silence," Gran demanded at last, in a voice that said she was not to be trifled with. "I will be the only one to speak to Peter from now on, do ye all understand? And then only to give him instructions as to where to turn. He is making a fine job of this driving, and Da will be proud of him. Drive on, my lad."

With that they were all silenced, except for the dog, whose moans continued—though more quietly—throughout the rest of the juggering ride.

It seemed to take forever, but at last they pulled up in front of the Eventide Home, close enough to the curb that the tires scraped.

Then they piled out of the car, like clowns in a circus routine, and headed directly for the front door.

■ ■ ■

This time no one greeted them. Indeed there seemed to be no one at home as they walked right through the two rooms toward the Garden Parlor. The Eventide Home was startlingly empty of residents. Even the old lady who had been sitting staring out at the road was gone.

"I will give that Maggie MacAlpin a piece of my mind," said Gran. "To think she has been my best friend forever, and never a word about her Pictish connections."

"But it was Mrs. McGregor who gave Molly the stone," Jennifer reminded her. "Not Mrs. MacAlpin."

"Then I will give them both a piece. And have a piece left over for Catriona Campbell as well. Yer not to practice witchcraft against yer friends. And never against members of yer own coven. Whatever did those three think they were doing? Or has the Eventide Home sapped them of their wits as well as their strength?"

There was no one in the Garden Parlor, either.

Just when Jennifer was sure something awful must have happened to the entire population of the Eventide Home—something to do with the dark mist, probably—there was a loud sound, rather like a flock of birds gabbling together. Along the hall, from the opposite end of the

Eventide Home, marched the residents in a ragged line.

"Och—lunchtime, of course," Gran said. "And now they've all been let out of the dining commons and are coming toward us like a gaggle of silly geese."

Since it was just what she'd been thinking herself, Jennifer started to laugh, as much in relief as anything else. Molly joined in, and so did Peter. Ninia laughed, too, though she had no idea what the others were finding so amusing.

But the dog made no such sound. Instead he backed up from the advancing line, tail between his legs, and found an improbable hiding place under the glass-topped table. There he began moaning, "Dark, dark, dark," till Peter gave him a slight kick.

Jennifer glanced out the window to the Eventide gardens and the cemetery wall beyond, fully expecting to see the dreaded dark mist advancing toward them. But the gardens were clear, the rain had stopped again, and it was sunshine that was now pouring down instead.

Molly began jumping around. "It's Fiona with them. See?" She pointed down the hall. "Do you think she'll have more ice cream for me, Gran? Can I ask her? Can I?"

Indeed it was Fiona, shepherding her flock with expert ease and infinite patience. Jennifer came to the doorway and watched as Fiona situated four old ladies on the sofa in one room and left them to their gossip. Then Fiona wheeled the old gentleman over to the fire to doze, though the fire was no longer lit. Next she pushed the lady in the wheelchair to the window and motioned at something, a bird, perhaps, or someone walking by. As she passed one of the fringed lampshades, she gave it a tweak with her fingers, her foxlike face looking slyer than ever.

Finally Fiona guided Gran's three friends—Mrs. McGregor, Mrs. Campbell, and Maggie Mac-Alpin—to the table at the Garden Parlor's Center.

"There, my dears," Fiona said. "Enjoy your card game." She tweaked the fringe on the shade by the table as well.

Ignoring the children, she added to Gran, "Perhaps you would like to play cards with them, Mrs. Douglas. And here's a shawl. You will get much too cold if you sit in here without one." Not waiting for permission this time, she placed the shawl over Gran's shoulders and smoothed it down.

"Perhaps..." Gran said slowly, as if trying to puzzle out something, "perhaps I would like to play." She sat in the empty chair. "And that shawl feels nice and warm."

"You miss your friends here in the Eventide Home, don't you," said Fiona. But it was less a question than a statement. "You should come more often. They need a fourth for the cards." She smiled and left the room.

"Play cards?" Jennifer said, appalled. "This is no time to play cards, Gran. I thought we came here to talk to Maggie MacAlpin. To give her a piece of your mind."

"About the Picts," Peter added.

Gran looked up a bit muzzily. "Of course we did, my dears. All in good time. Canna rush these things. All in good time. These are my friends. I miss them. I should come more often. They need a fourth for the cards."

"What picks do you want to talk to me about, Gwen?" Maggie's hair was standing up around her head like a hatful of orange wires. "Are ye into horse racing now? Or is it a pick for the coming football matches?"

"About..." Gran began, then faltered.

"About you and Kenneth mac Alpin, the king," Jennifer blurted out. "The one who..." She tried to remember the exact wording, then had it at last. "Who forged together a single nation of Scots and Picts."

"Och, weel, that was a long time ago," Maggie MacAlpin said. "Auld Kenneth, as we call him. We've nae claim to the crown noo." She picked up the cards and began to deal.

■ ■ ■

Fiona came back with some ice cream for each of the children, and Peter and Molly dug into theirs with great gusto. Ninia tried to imitate them, but when she picked up the spoon she dropped it at once with a cry and shook out her hand.

"Too hot for you, too cold for me," Jennifer said, putting her bowl down.

"Eat it," said Fiona. Her voice, which had been soft and persuasive before, now seemed full of a terrible threat. "Eat your ice cream."

Jennifer gritted her teeth until they hurt. "I... don't... like... ice... cream," she said.

"It's nae ice and never cream," cried the dog

from beneath the table. "It's a wee bit o' the dark. Leave it be."

It was clear that Fiona had not been expecting the dog to speak, and for a moment she was stunned. But only for a moment. Raising her right hand, she pointed at him and cried out a single awful word. The word was as loud as a gunshot and just as deafening. For a moment everything stopped, just like a movie's freeze-action frame, Jennifer thought.

The dog leaped up as if burned, upsetting the table and the deck of cards, overturning a lamp, and bumping into Jennifer, who fell heavily to the floor. Then he ran from the room yelping.

Ninia put her hands over her ears. The four old women looked strangely dazed. Ninia hadn't moved since the dog had scampered away. And Peter and Molly seemed frozen in place by the sound of Fiona's magic word, or by the ice cream, or both.

Do something, Jennifer tried to tell herself. *Do something now.* But for the life of her, she didn't know what to do.

FIFTEEN

Power

Fiona began to smile. That smile reminded Jennifer of the wizard Michael Scot. There was no real joy behind it and it never reached her eyes. It was a serpent's smile, all lips and no teeth.

"Do not even think of getting up, little American," Fiona said to Jennifer. "Ye canna stand against me. I have gathered all the power from these auld carlines to me. I have silenced the boy and the little lassies. And yer gran's power, as soon as I gather it up, will make me stronger still."

"But why?" Jennifer asked, her voice barely a whisper. Gran had said that *why* was the question to ask of magic. Also, if she could keep Fiona talking, someone—anyone—might come to their rescue. At least it always worked like that in the movies.

"Why?" Fiona laughed. "Because these auld

wives do not know when it is time enough to die. Why should they have all the power, and we young ones have to wait? *Stay quiet,* my teachers told me. *Study hard. And maybe*—when I'm fifty years or so—*ye will have the knowledge and the power.* Well, I dinna want to wait that long. Till I am fifty and dried up, with lines in my face and a kernel for a heart. I dinna want to wait—and now I dinna have to."

"But what you're doing is wrong," Jennifer said hoarsely.

"Wrong is only right from the other side," said Fiona. "And how can it be right for the auld to hold on to power?"

"Maybe it has to do with...wisdom?" asked Jennifer cautiously.

Fiona laughed. "And how wise are these auld carlines, putting themselves in my hands? They already forget the words to spells. They give away objects of magic without thinking. With their crabbed auld hands, they cannna tie a solid elf-knot. Those things have naught to do wi' wisdom, my lass."

"But..." Everything Fiona was saying was wrong. Jennifer felt that in her bones. So she tried to think of another argument. She could feel something else wrong, too, though she didn't tell Fiona. In fact, she was lying on the something wrong and it was poking hard into her backside and hurt like crazy. She tried to wriggle away from it, but it seemed to scooch along with her whichever way she moved.

"Stop moving about, ye stupid Yank," said Fiona. "Ye'll not be pulling any American tricks on me."

"I'm just trying to get comfortable," complained Jennifer, willing herself to whine, making herself sound weaker than she was. She wished Peter could help. Fiona needed a swift karate kick to the knees! "What's wrong with that?"

"*Wrong...wrong...*ye keep harping on the word," said Fiona. "From where I stand, what I am doing is right. And I have the *right* to hurt ye, if ye don't stop that infernal wriggling."

Jennifer stopped wriggling and quickly changed the subject. "Look at them," she said, nodding at the four women at the table. "Surely you're not doing right by them, no matter where you stand."

"Are they hurt?" asked Fiona. "Do they want for anything? They are well fed and well clothed and kept dry and warm. Dinna ye watch the news, little Yank? Dinna ye ken how people are starving in Africa and in Pakistan and in parts of the States as well? These auld folk are happy here. They can play their little games at the table, and even think they are ordering me around. Still, it's I who have the power noo, nae those auld carlines."

Power, thought Jennifer. *It always comes down to that.*

Fiona smiled, and this time it seemed genuine. "I want you to notice, lass, that though I have taken their power from them, I *willna* have them hurt."

"But it's *your* will—not theirs," Jennifer said. "They've had no say in the matter."

"Aye—my will. And my time, too. For the power." Fiona's voice was triumphant.

It's not like the movies after all, Jennifer thought. *The bad guy has talked and talked and in all that time no one has come to rescue us.* She knew then that any rescue was going to be up to her. Yet time was running out and she didn't have even the beginning of a plan.

Still, whatever she was lying on hurt more than ever. The first thing she'd have to do was get rid of it. She began feeling around, but carefully this time, so as not to annoy Fiona. At last she managed to pull out what she had been lying on. It was the overturned lamp's electric cord. Unaccountably, the three-pronged plug seemed to leap into her hand.

"Enough gassing," Fiona said. "Time for ye to shut yer cake hole, and listen carefully. I'll not hurt ye, nor yer brother nor yer sister and her strange little friend, either. But ye will have to forget what has happened here. It would hae been better if ye had eaten the ice cream." She fingered the little silver scissors that hung on the ribbon around her neck. "I can make ye forget. I have ways. And they willna hurt. No more than I've hurt these auld dears."

Going over to Molly, Fiona began to twist several locks of the little girl's curls together. "Do ye see—the ice cream froze her natural resistance. So noo I can easily tie just three elfknots into little Molly Isabelle's hair. Och—yes, I have her name. The auld dears told me. It will make the spell all that much tighter, and she'll nae remember a thing after. I have always been good at knotwork. In fact, anything to do with yarn. Even before I kenned about the Craft, as we call witchery here in Scotland." She spoke with a casualness that belied the wickedness she was doing. "And then I discovered that the black arts have a use for it, the yarn skill. To call a wind, to send a flux, to take someone into yer power."

Jennifer stared at Fiona with growing horror. The young woman looked so normal, so nice as she fiddled with Molly's curls. Yet what she was really doing was so wicked. Jennifer shuddered. Then she glanced at the shawl over Gran's shoulders, with its tasseled fringes tied in intricate knots.

What was it Gran said about elfknots? Then Jennifer had it: Their power depended on the magic-maker's intentions.

Well, she knew Fiona's intentions, all right—and they weren't good. The knots on the shawl over Gran's shoulders had sapped her of her natural power. Jennifer thought that if she could just somehow get over and pull the shawl off of Gran, then Gran could battle Fiona for them all.

Slowly Jennifer sat up.

But Fiona saw the movement and turned. "Dinna try me," she said, lifting one finger from her work. She had already tied the second elfknot and was beginning the third. "Dinna think to try me. Ye Americans—ye have nae power."

That was when Jennifer remembered Gran's voice clearly saying, *Scots have power, but Americans have . . .*

She hoped it would work. She knew herself untrained in magic; indeed, she hadn't even believed in magic before they'd come to Scotland and battled Michael Scot. Still—she had to *try.* There was no one else. The old ladies and Gran were caught by the magic shawls, Peter and Molly frozen by the ice cream, Ninia stunned by all that had happened. It was *really* up to Jennifer now.

She moved the hand that held the three-pronged plug, held it in front of her like a weapon, and pointed it at Fiona.

"No power, maybe," Jennifer said, "but we *do* have electricity!"

Focusing entirely on the hand holding the plug, Jennifer made herself think of electrons rising up inside her. *My hand is a conduit,* she thought. *I am a conductor.* She raised her hand for a magical downbeat.

And suddenly arcing through her body was a

surge of electric power that ran down her arm and into the cord. She could feel it, like a great tingling sensation all over. Then the electricity leaped out of the plug in three separate shining strands, to strike right at the center of the silver scissors lying on Fiona's breast.

The shock hit Fiona with such power she was knocked backward across the room and bang up against the wall. Falling to the floor in a heap, she lay without moving.

"Out like a light," Jennifer said, trying to stand but suddenly so weak she could not get up off her knees. "An electric light!" She giggled, not out of amusement but out of pure relief.

The dog came galloping back into the room. "Did it work?" he cried. "Did it work? I remembered the elfknots on the lampshades. So I scampered out of here and knocked them over and chewed through as many as I could... Ye should see the auld dears moving aboot in there. They have much of their auld energy back."

"And maybe," Jennifer added, "their power." All she wanted to do was to sleep. But they had no time for that, so instead she pointed to where Fiona lay on the floor.

The dog loped over to the fallen Fiona. He sniffed her head to toe, then back again, and looked up. "What's this? What's this? Nae the knots, then?"

Jennifer stood slowly and went over to the table. She lifted the shawl from Gran's shoulders and felt a rush of foreign power under her fingers.

"I expect you weakened Fiona a lot, otherwise what I did wouldn't have worked." She wasn't sure she believed that, but she was not sure *what* she believed anymore.

"Weel, I did that. I did," the dog said. But—"

Jennifer shrugged. Then she took the shawls off the other three women as well, feeling the power once again, a strange, eerie tingling. She threw the shawls in a far corner, where for a moment they shimmered, then went dim. "But what?"

"But *ye* finished her off," the dog said.

For a moment Jennifer went cold. "Finished her off? Do you mean that she's dead? I didn't mean to kill her. I didn't know I had such—"

"Power? Aye, that ye do, lass. Though ye may call it sommat else."

"How will we explain this to the police?"

The dog chuckled, tiring of his joke. "She's nae

dead. But she'll nae remember a thing of her black magic noo. The shock was too great."

Jennifer sighed and felt a weight lifting from her shoulders. "How did you guess about the knots?"

"The nose kens all," he said, giving a large sniff. "And I recalled that Pictish child plaiting elfknots in Devil's mane."

"Or maybe," Jennifer said slowly, "you were just listening to us at the door."

The dog grinned and showed a mouthful of yellow teeth.

"And all that while I lay in agony on that electric cord," Jennifer said. "Why didn't you help?"

"I'm just a dog, ye gormless fool, nae a wizard. I have nae hands! Besides, ye were doing just fine wi'oot me. Now get those knots oot of yer sister's hair," he said. "I'd try it myself but I'd make a sopping mess of it."

"You would, indeed." Jennifer laughed and Peter, who was already coming around from the ice-cream freeze, laughed with her.

Just then Gran shook herself all over. There was a light back in her eyes. "Maggie MacAlpin," she said, as if no time at all had passed since she'd sat down, "I need a word with ye."

"More than one, I'll wager," said Maggie. "Ye were always a laiging lass."

"It's not gossip I want to talk about," Gran said. "It's about the Picts and Auld Kenneth and a horrible dark mist."

SIXTEEN

Journey Home

Before they could speak of the mist and Pictish history, Fiona stood up, shaking her head as if she had lost something. She was a bit misty herself, both apologetic for having forgotten to bring them all their tea and also wondering how she came to be so sore.

"It's as if something has gone and struck me right here in the chest," she said, pointing to the silver scissors.

Jennifer saw that there was a half-moon shape cut out of one of the blades. The remembered power made her fingers feel all pins and needles.

"Now, who would be doing any such thing?" Gran asked sweetly. "It may be a colic coming on."

"I have just the thing for that," said Mrs. Campbell, standing up and taking Fiona by the arm. "In my room."

"And she does, too," said Mrs. McGregor. "A dab hand is our Catriona with the herbs." She followed them out.

"Not as dab as our Gwen," said Maggie MacAlpin, smiling.

"Ye'll not fob us off with a smile," said Gran. "Noo, first I'm going to tell ye what happened to us, and then, Maggie, it will be yer turn." She recited the events of the day, starting with the giving of the stone.

Maggie MacAlpin looked grey. "That stone," she said. "It was mine to give, not Susan McGregor's."

"I thought as much." Gran nodded her head.

"But . . ." Maggie MacAlpin mused, ". . . if Fiona had gotten her hands on the stone . . ."

Jennifer gasped, thinking about Fiona rummaging through time and concentrating centuries of magic in her own hands. Like the wizard Michael Scot, but without his vast knowledge. She couldn't decide which would have been worse.

Maggie spoke again. "That stone was brought through time, hand to hand, one MacAlpin woman to the next. I got it from my ain mother."

"Fancy that," said Gran.

"But, as ye ken," Maggie said, "I hae nae daughters of my ain."

Jennifer leaned forward. "Taken..." she whispered. "Waken. Mistaken. Shaken..."

Maggie MacAlpin turned toward Jennifer so fast, pins scattered from her orange hair. "How do ye ken those words, lass?"

"Why?" asked Jennifer.

Gran smiled. "Jennifer has the right of it, Maggie, and weel ye ken it."

Maggie MacAlpin shook her head. "I dinna *ken* the why of it. Only the spell. It's been called 'The Chant of the Stone,' and all firstborn MacAlpin girls learn it."

"Say it," said Gran. "Say it to us noo."

"I canna, Gwen. Yer nae a MacAlpin."

Gran raised her right forefinger. "I'm nae wanting to bid ye, Maggie. We hae been friends too lang for that. But I will if I must, and weel ye ken it."

Maggie bit her lower lip. "Time is out of joint," she said.

"And ye put it that way, ye muckle auld witch," cried the dog.

Maggie silenced him with a glance.

"*Taken* . . ." Jennifer said again. "That's not right. Magic must be given, not taken. Gran told us that on our very first day here."

"What's *lost* is not taken," Maggie said. "What's found is given." Then she put her head back, closed her eyes, and spoke a verse in a quavering voice that made the hairs on Jennifer's neck stand on end.

> *What be lost can noo be taken.*
> *Mists of time will all awaken.*
> *Wrongs and errors long mistaken*
> *Noo from time can all be shaken.*

Peter, who was now finally and fully warmed up, shook his head. "That makes no sense," he said. "It's just a bunch of rhymed words."

"They make every bit of sense," said Gran.

Jennifer smiled. "*What be lost can now be taken* is simple. It means the talisman, of course. Lost in the garden, taken up by Mrs. McGregor, and given to Molly before Fiona could get her hands on it."

"Exactly," Gran said, smiling at Jennifer.

"And we know the mists of time have awakened.

You"—Jennifer pointed at Peter—"even let them in twice."

"I didn't mean to," Peter grumbled. "No need to remind me. Not you, Jen." He turned away.

But as they were talking, the dark had begun to gather again. It was Ninia who noticed it first. Since she hadn't understood a word they were saying, she'd been gazing through the window and drawing Pictish symbols with her finger on the glass.

Suddenly she gave a cry and pointed toward the cemetery. It did not sound like a cry of fear or terror. Rather she seemed sad. Even lonely.

"She's homesick," Molly announced.

"But her home is many centuries away," Gran told Molly.

"And full of wars. And people dying," added Jennifer.

"The world is *still* full of wars," Peter said, with irritating logic. "So she ought to feel right at home here."

But Molly answered with irrefutable four-year-old reasoning, "Even with wars. Back then is her home."

Jennifer clapped her hand over her mouth. "Oh!" she said.

"What is it, lass?" Gran asked.

"*Wrongs and errors long mistaken.* Could that mean what happened when the Scots killed all the Pictish leaders? We read about it in the museum. Maybe we're meant to go back and shake things out of time and change them so that the Picts win."

"And *poof!*" said Peter scornfully. "*We'd* all go out like a light. All the *good* things done by Scots through the ages would disappear as well."

"Like what?" asked Molly.

"Like kilts and bagpipes and tartans and golf," said Jennifer.

"Like Watt and the steam engine," said Peter. "Like McAdam and paved streets. Like Bell and the telephone. Like..." They all suddenly stared at him. He shrugged. "I like reading about science stuff."

"It's the Scot in ye," Gran said, smiling.

"That's all well and good," the dog said, "but how do ye get Ninia back? The stone is gone, tied up in a knot in Devil's mane."

"Only we call him Thunder and Night now," Molly put in.

"A knot in the de'il's mane," said Mrs. McGregor. "Well, well, well, and here's a lot to ponder."

"And no time to ponder it in," said Gran. "The mist is already here. I suspect that it can take the child back with or without the stone."

Maggie MacAlpin stood. "I have had long enough, my dears, for my pondering. Here's what I be thinking. Fiona, puir lass, didna go about things correctly, but she had the right of it nonetheless. Nae a one of us kens when it's time to give o'er our power. Nor do we ken the moment when we are to die. But seven or eight is surely too young, I'm thinking, as Ninia here must have been when she died in the past. And killed by my own kinsman, too. All because he feared her child to come. Well, I dinna like it and I willna have it! Surely the Chant passed down through time means that none of the other MacAlpin women have liked it, either. That stone was to remind us that one day one of us women with enough wisdom must go back and change things. Not to give victory to the Picts. That's a man's solution. But to make the Scots more just, which is a woman's way. And if Kenneth mac Alpin will listen to this auld carline, I will give him an earful." She grinned. "And some advice on ruling, too."

"What do ye mean, Maggie?" Gran asked.

"Why, the Pictish lass and I will be going home together," Maggie said. "Back through the centuries. To Pictland."

"Pictland's not yer home, Maggie," cried Gran.

"Nor is this, Gwen," Maggie said, gesturing around her.

She went over to Ninia and touched her on the head. "Come, dearie." Then without a word more, she opened the garden door and—leading Ninia by the hand—walked across the rolled lawn toward the mist.

"Gran," Jennifer cried, "you have to stop them!"

"Maggie MacAlpin always was full of herself," said Gran. There were tears running down her cheeks. She didn't wipe them away.

As they watched through the window, the dark mist greeted Ninia and Maggie, not as if they were enemies, but like old friends. It wrapped itself around them and—in an instant—they were gone.

Seventeen

After

Jennifer flung the door open and started after them. By the time she got to the gate, the mist was gone as well.

"What happened, Jennifer?" asked Molly, who had followed her and was now swinging on the gate. "What happened to my Ninia?"

"I don't know," Jennifer said. "I just don't know." Her voice tore, like cloth on a nail.

Peter came up behind them. "The mist—it's not anywhere."

"Or anytime," added the dog, sniffing. "The nose kens all."

Molly jumped off the gate and ran into the cemetery, toward the oak where the Pictish graves lay.

"Wait!" Jennifer called. "Molly! It might still be dangerous!"

The dog sniffed the air again. "Definitely gone," he said. "Let the bairn run."

Still they all chased after her and when they caught up, she was down on her knees under the tree. "Look, Jen! Look, Peter! Look, dog!"

They looked. And Gran, who had caught up with them, looked as well.

The three large graves were still there, undisturbed. But of the littlest grave, there was no sign.

Gran smiled. "She gave Auld Kenneth an earful, indeed. That Maggie MacAlpin always was a good talker."

■ ■ ■

They left the car in front of the Eventide Home and walked back to the cottage. There was a light scattering of rain, but no one seemed to mind it.

"Da can drive the car back himself," said Gran. "I think that's safer."

They all agreed, and Peter seemed the most relieved.

"I'd probably have driven it right through the garage wall." He was actually grinning.

"Through the door first," added the dog, "and

then into the wall. Ye have an uneven foot on that pedal."

"I dinna think so, Peter dear," said Gran. "I wouldna let ye."

"*Let* me?"

"Were you keeping us safe all the way along, Gran?" asked Molly. "With magic?"

"Let's just say," Gran told her, "that I was praying mighty hard for the lad. Uneven foot and all. If it's mechanical magic he has, he's nae quite grown into it yet."

Jennifer nodded. "Boys *do* mature later than girls," she said.

"Later than dogs as well," said the dog. He braced himself for a yank on the leash.

But Peter just laughed. "Gran—I hope you'll come to America in three years."

"Why three exactly?" asked Gran. "Be it a magical number, ye mean?"

"It's when I take my driving test," Peter said. "And Scottish magic then—well, it couldn't hurt."

■ ■ ■

Peter and Molly were sent out to the garden to straighten up the mess they'd left, and the dog followed close behind. To their astonishment, there was the horse, contentedly cropping the grass, his once-glossy coat matted with sweat.

"I thought ye were off fighting battles," said the dog. "Winning wars. Blowing into Pictish noses. Snuffling hotly into their hands."

"And quite a battle it was, too. It went on for many long hours."

"Really?" Peter asked.

"And since when does a horse have any sense of time?" muttered the dog. "Carry a clock, do ye?"

The horse pointedly ignored him. "Well, many long minutes, anyway. Those weapons are heavy, you know. Blow after blow after—"

"Enough blowing!" moaned the dog. "Get on wi' it."

The horse shook his head. "Some folk have no sense of story."

"Story, yes—but yer making it a history," said the dog. "With nae beginning and nae end, only lots of middle."

"Please go on, Thunder," Peter said softly. "With the story. We really want to know."

"*Really!*" Molly added.

Thunder nodded, obviously pleased with his

new name. He grinned, showing large yellow teeth. "For you, Peter, and you, Molly, I will continue the tale. But not for him." He lifted his head toward the dog, who was now studying his paws. "*He* is a Philistine and a boor."

Molly clapped her hands. "Go on! Go on!"

The horse cleared its throat. "When at last the Scots champion slammed Bridei with the butt end of his spear..." The horse paused. "And a false blow that was, I can tell you." He sniffed loudly. "Poor Bridei slipped off my back and, falling, pulled loose the stone in my mane."

"On purpose?" asked Peter.

"Or accident?" asked Molly.

"Does it matter a whit?" asked the dog.

The horse ignored them all, deep into his own story. "And then Bridei was gone, into the dark mist, and the mist gone with him. I had been tied to them and to time by that knotted stone, and when it was undone, I returned here. To the garden. With naught to do but wait for you."

"A likely story," said the dog, scratching himself. "And much too complicated."

"It *has* to be true," said Molly. "Thunder's all sweaty. And look—some of his mane's been pulled out." She patted the horse on his neck and he turned his head back to nuzzle the top of Molly's hair.

"Och—and another fine display, that," complained the dog. "Do not, I beg ye, Mistress Molly, blow in his nose. It only encourages him."

But Molly, taking the dog's complaint as some kind of dare, pulled the horse's head down till his nostrils were even with her mouth and blew.

■ ■ ■

Meanwhile Jennifer was helping in the kitchen. "Do you think Ninia lived to grow up? To get married? To have babies? To be a queen?"

Gran put her head to one side, considering. "It was probably Ninia as a grown-up, remembering what was to happen in the future, and carefully taught by Maggie, who sent that stone through history in the hands of MacAlpin women, till it reached here centuries later."

"Whoosh!" said Jennifer. "Like a snake swallowing its tail! She lived here and so, with Maggie's help, knew in the past what to do to make the future safe."

Gran smiled. "Yer quick, my lass. I'm pleased with ye."

Jennifer beamed.

"Ninia certainly didna die young," Gran continued. "There was no grave in the cemetery for her. And there's *always* been a child's grave there, as far back as I can remember—which is very far, indeed." She handed Jennifer a towel for drying.

"I'm glad," said Jennifer. "Though it seems strange to be happy about something that happened hundreds and hundreds of years ago. I mean—however Ninia's life turned out, it's in the way far past."

"We are *all* someone else's past," said Gran. She began to wash the dishes. The white cat suddenly appeared in the doorway and came over to twine around her legs.

Jennifer considered what Gran had said for a long moment, wondering whose past *she* could possibly be.

"Gran . . ." Jennifer at last said slowly. "What do you think the dark mist was?"

"Concentrated history," said Gran, handing Jennifer a dish. "And tied somehow to the little stone, the focus of MacAlpin power. When the stone was given to Molly and then you took it up with your raw, untrained American magic, that history began to unravel and Ninia got flung forward to knit it up again."

"To get the stone?"

"To get what the stone was sent for, hand to hand over the years."

"Then it was a race, really, between the stone's wishes and the mist's wishes?"

"Something like that," said Gran, handing more dishes to Jennifer. "Though neither stone nor mist actually wished anything. It was Ninia's wish—the grown-up Ninia's, as well as the child's—that used both stone and mist to get what was needed. The stone to change things, the mist to open the gates of time."

"And Bridei?" Jennifer said, swiping at the dishes with her cloth.

Gran sighed. "Ah—Bridei. I think Ninia hoped when he appeared that he might win. But she was taking no chances. He had lost before in the past, so why should he win here? She sent herself into the future, her child self, and Bridei simply followed." Gran turned off the faucet and dried her hands.

"So the past got more than it bargained for," Jennifer said.

"Och—aye, that it certainly did. It got Maggie MacAlpin." She suddenly put her apron over her eyes, and her shoulders shook.

Jennifer set the dishes down and went over to Gran and hugged her. "Don't cry, Gran. I know Maggie's having a good time. Surely better than in the Eventide Home."

"Och, I ken that, all right," said Gran. "But I am going to miss her sorely. We've been the best of friends since childhood, and noo she's gone away. As far away as ever she could."

"And you wish she were back?"

"Maybe I just wish I were with her!" said Gran. She dried her eyes with the apron. "And dinna ye be telling Da I said so, or I'll have a year of explaining to do."

Just then they heard a key turning in the lock. "Speak of the auld de'il himself," said Gran. "What a story we shall have at tea!"

And they did, too, though no one quite believed it. Not even themselves.

A Scottish Glossary

aboot—about

ain—own

auld—old

bairn—child

besom—unpleasant woman

blether—nonsense

bricht—beautiful (as in a beautiful woman)

brolly—umbrella

canna—cannot

carline—old woman, witch

clan—one's extended family

crisps—potato chips

cummer—witch

dab—light, soft, fine

daft—crazy

de'il—devil

didna—did not

dinna—do not

dreech—wet, dreary

fash—bother, annoy

fob—to palm (off) something

glundie—a fool

gomeril—loud-talking fool

gormless—stupid

greetin—crying, weeping

greetin teenie—someone who is always
    complaining

haar—a sea mist

hae—have

havering—going on and on about something

hokeypokey—ice cream; hocus pocus

honk—throw up, vomit

keep us—God keep us safe

ken—know

kin—relatives

lad, laddie—a boy

laiging—gossiping

lang—long

lass, lassie—a girl or young woman

midden—dung heap

muckle—great

nae—not, no

nain—none

noo—now

puir—poor

sommat—somewhat, something

tea—can be used to mean supper

wardrobe—a stand-alone closet

wee—little, very little

wee, sleekit, cowrin, tim'rous—from the Robert Burns poem "To a Mouse," it means "small, sleek, cowering, frightened"

weel—well

wellies—short for "Wellingtons," rubber boots

willna—will not

wi'oot—without